THE GHOST IN THE GRASS

MT ROBERTS

ABERRANT LITERATURE

THE GHOST IN THE GRASS

Published by Aberrant Literature

Copyright © 2020 by MT Roberts

Cover Art *"Rynth Residence" oil on canvas, by Matt Roberts*

www.aberrantliterature.com

ISBN 978-1-953312-05-1 Paperback Edition

ISBN 978-1-953312-07-5 Hardcover Edition

ISBN 978-1-953312-06-8 Digital Edition

for Ashes

Chapter One

South Africa
June, 1903

JOHAN CLOSED HIS POCKET WATCH AND LET HIS GAZE DRIFT TO THE window. In the distance stood the bent outline of a withered mokala tree, fingering the horizon, a lone sentinel of endless dust and heat moving stark and slow beneath the sky. It soon retreated behind a line of hills, leaving Johan with nothing to look at save an old man's tired reflection. He pinched the bridge of his nose and pulled his glasses down, rubbing his eyes. The earthen tones and glaring sunlight were beginning to have an effect on him. Reaching into his coat for his pipe, he paused at the feel of Karl's letter. Johan rasped at its worn edges, hesitant.

The train gave a moan, shaking as it took a curve in the Karoo. Johan clutched at his table in the open booth, feeling a warm draft toddle up the aisle of the car. He closed his eyes and leaned back, allowing the mixture of excitement and dread rising within him to compound among the shuddering luggage racks and quivering windowpanes. How long had it been? Almost thirty years? Johan flared his nostrils. The journey to Port Elizabeth alone had taken him over three weeks by ship. Due to the hordes of demobilized Englishmen filling the railways, procuring passage to De Aar had been an affair all its own, but what really agitated him were his telegrams to Karl, none of which garnered a response. Johan supposed this should have been expected. After all, it was just like Karl to ask the difficult, then leave its doing to someone else. Johan relaxed his grip on the ossified table. Despite his misgivings, he was here on the last leg of the trip, and visiting Karl would be good; Sylvia had wanted them to make amends.

The engine's whistle let out a scream—a lingering pitch lost to the russet expanse. Thick smoke billowed by Johan's row of windows, shadowing the dirty upholstery and tarnished fixtures inside. Even through the incessant rattling of the tracks, through the sporadic lurching and whining of the empty car, Karl's letter tapped at Johan's chest, pricking at him, needling him through his shirt. In the dark of the smoke, Johan acquiesced and slipped the envelope from his coat pocket, turning it over in his hands, rubbing his thumb over the font of Karl's typewriter. Postmarked from the British Cape Colony on the Third of March, it was sent off almost a month to the day before Sylvia's funeral. Johan upended the yellow flap and pulled Karl's letter to the table:

Johan,

I know you hold contempt for me. I know I should have worked harder to clear my name all those years ago. I know my absence was a token of infidelity to our long friendship, and for that, I am deserving of your contempt— but overall, I know you. And so, I ask for your help once again. Several months ago, I discovered a wonder in the savanna here—the Karoo, they call it. Old friend, it changes everything we thought. Absolutely everything. I wish I could give you more information, but, as of yet, I am unsure of even my own friends in this region, what with the British and Afrikaners having only recently put their feud behind them. And unfortunately, my position as a land surveyor does not grant me immunity from the eager capitalists and prying governors here.

Please come. Bring Hendrik if you would? We could use his eye. And bring as many men as the society can spare, if at all possible. Just be sparse about what you say to them.

I have included what I believe to be ample pence for you and Hendrik to come by ship. You would be wise to sail straight through for the Cape and ignore our colony to the West, as getting a train to De Aar from Otijimbingue might cause issue with the Schutztruppen. They are on point as of late, following the end of Krueger and his ilk.

My friend, haste is advised. Be cautious of what you impart to strangers, as suspicion is rampant here. The easting and northing of my location is attached.

Please hurry, as I hope to see you both very soon.

- K. Rynth
PS Give her my regards?

Johan laced his fingers together, overcome with the same deflated sensation as before, when he first read the letter, alone in his study a week after Sylvia's passing. Of course, Karl had no way of knowing Sylvia had been ill, but his lack of awareness stung all the same—it made apparent just how wide the gulf between them had grown throughout the years. Johan cleared his throat and returned the letter to its envelope. Watching the black smoke play at the windows, he rolled Karl's words over in his head—just what exactly did Karl think this discovery of his changed? And to request of the Deutsche Orient-Gesellschaft that it send an expedition to the Orange! Risible. The volunteer aspect of the society's archaeological reach was only five years old and certainly not interested in Karl Rynth's nebulous findings somewhere in South Africa. The man had been disgraced decades ago; he held no clout.

Sunlight seeped into the tattered murk of the car, the engine's smoke rising as the train eased off its curve in the tracks. Johan readjusted himself and retrieved his pipe, fingering its sooted bowl with an absent interest, tapping it out on the table, overcome with guilt that the scattered ashes should remind him of his wife. He swiped the gray particles onto the dirty rug in the aisle and pictured

Sylvia's urn back home in Berlin. Maybe he should have brought Hendrik after all.

And why not? Hendrik was a capable young man, if not a little stoic at times. The boy had, in fact, been so stone-faced that Johan often joked he should have been delivered by a general instead of a nurse and put right in the ranks! Hendrik would have done well in the military—there was no doubt of that—but the boy's pursuit of archaeology had so pleased Johan, and who was he to get in the way of legacy? Smirking at the image of his son in uniform, Johan unfurled his tobacco pouch and packed the bowl of his pipe, leaving any thoughts of Sylvia with the ashes on the rug.

He struck a match and pulled at the flame, focused on the muted crackle of roasting tobacco—a sound usually calming to him, now dulled by the clatter of train tracks and uneven windowpanes. With a flick of his wrist, he extinguished the match and narrowed his eyes as a huddle of white buildings rose on the horizon beyond a series of low, grassy hills. Johan exhaled through his nostrils, following the curled rise of blue smoke as it crawled along the windowpane, eager for escape.

A loud clank resounded as the cabin door slid open. Johan withdrew his cane from the luggage rack and tidied his table, unsure of the muffled conversations outside. With a considerable wince, he stood and watched as people shuffled along the windows, shouting to one another and coughing. Why were so many lined up for the train? And with so many belongings? Cautious of the bunched rug in the aisle, Johan made his way through the car, studying the crowd. It seemed the majority of them were sick—likely a bout of summer flu.

Johan pulled on the brim of his hat and stepped carefully to the white concrete outside, gripping his stick for support. The chatter around him dulled to a murmur in the sun—a murmur suffused with anxieties and feverish whispers. Johan frowned, leaning harder into his cane. Why did no one approach him? Where was Karl?

A wooden 'clack' on the concrete behind him broke the uneasy quiet—Johan's traveling trunk had been unloaded from the train to the platform by an unseen porter. The crowd moved in to swarm the passenger car as Johan dragged his chest out of the way. Panting, he eyed the dark engine on its tracks, furled with rising thermals like some prehistoric beast, and imagined the clamoring locals as a rush of carrion ants, ravenous and eager to penetrate its hard shell. Johan rubbed his temple, trying to tolerate the sun. His brown sack suit wafted in the heat, pungent from travel. How did these people accept such temperature?

Johan watched a moment as the people handed their belongings to a group of men atop the passenger car, tired from lugging his trunk through the funneling din. Surely someone had come to pick him up; he just needed to find them and make himself known. Johan wiped his brow and maneuvered the morass of black and white faces, limping with his luggage through the fervid strangers that hacked and coughed and yelled in Afrikaans. When a cream-plastered stairway led him to a crude dirt path, he stepped aside and surveyed the town before him, relieved at the open space. A breeze off the Karoo spun clouds of dust as bright as turmeric across his shoes. Inhaling the scent of dried grass, Johan took a seat on his trunk and waited.

The station-town sat perhaps a hundred meters from the railway platform, surrounded entirely by a waist-high border of white plastered stonework. It bore the usual squat design of British colonialism—low buildings set to either side of a single manicured avenue, the highest roof a dome adorned with a tattered Union Jack. Johan pursed his lips, absorbed for the first time in the reality of Karl's choices of life and home. It was all so beneath him; this station-town represented just how far Karl had tumbled since his days in the society.

Johan gazed at the immensity of the Karoo and its undaunted openness. In the foothills stood the emaciated profile of two quiver trees—thick, buoyant bones adrift in a sea of burnt grass. The screech of a goshawk startled him, and Johan returned his attention to the station-town. A group of soldiers walked in his direction—no doubt, the tardy escort sent to retrieve him.

Standing up straight, Johan put his hands in his pockets and nodded with a friendly smile as the soldiers neared. They were a shambling regiment of tired men with uneven faces covered in a few days worth of beard, their uniforms more of a canary brown than khaki. Expecting to hear one of them offer an apology on Karl's behalf, Johan was confused to find they paid him no regard. Instead, they merely passed him by and crested the platform's steps, disappearing into the crowd. Had Karl really sent no one to pick him up? Was he not to have an escort? His face a rictus of disbelief, Johan scanned the outskirts of the station-town. In the distance, he spotted a large tent in the afternoon haze, beyond the town proper, and if he squinted, he could make out a few hunched figures drinking on a bench before its fluttering canvas. Johan licked his lips and dragged his trunk across the dirt. Maybe Karl was in there, beating the heat with a pint.

Johan made his way to the waist-high border wall of the station-town and scuffled alongside it. The pale wooden houses packed beside the main avenue were basic constructs—practical and matching, yet devoid of any personal touch. He supposed the crowd at the platform answered this—a mass exodus. But if everyone was so intent on departing, how would the town continue? An influx of new arrivals would be needed for the station-town's survival. So why had he been the only passenger on the train?

Johan wiped at his forehead as he approached the tent. It was a spiraled Outfitter three meters high with tall bronze stakes contorted about its base. He realized the men drinking at the benches were also soldiers—off duty, by the looks of their untucked uniforms. The soldiers raised their heads to appraise him as Johan walked by, tilting his hat in greeting. He noticed the cups of gin in their hands and grew eager to step inside for one of his own. Johan parted the canvas flaps and ducked through, feeling much-needed shade wash over him.

The tent smelled of mold and lamp oil, its entirety filled with an assortment of goods and burlap. Toward the back, past a pair of wooden posts, a large portion of canvas folded to allow a view of the Karoo. A warm breeze swayed inside, scattering the straw at the floor. Johan focused on the small table with its pair of mismatched chairs set just before the angling sunlight.

"Day."

Johan turned to a man behind a makeshift bar of stacked crates. He was young and gaunt, rubbing a tin mug with a dirty rag.

"Just off the engine?" The young man's voice was pregnant with a cold. He wiped his nose with the rag.

"Hello," Johan said. "Ja, I've just arrived from De Aar—ah, vergib mir, I'm Dr. Johan Mannswell." Johan left his trunk near the wavering flaps and walked over, extending his hand. The young man took it with limp fingers, his eyes damp and set a little too close together.

"Thomas Dawls."

"Mr. Dawls, ja—yes. Mr. Dawls, I'm afraid I feel a bit lost." Johan smiled. "You see, I was supposed to be greeted by an old colleague of mine. Perhaps you know of him, where I might find him? He was the land surveyor for your station-town. Mr. Karl Rynth?"

Johan knew Thomas weighed his German accent and was eyeing him with careful calculation.

"You here about the sick?" Thomas asked, rubbing the tin mug. "I heard Governor Tuner was in talks to bring outside help. Awful business, that."

"I'm afraid I don't know anything about it. No, Mr. Rynth is a friend. I was supposed to meet him."

Thomas's bloodless lips squirmed above his chin. "Well, I haven't seen him for some time. Suppose he's somewhere, though I don't think he stays in town too often."

"I see." Johan brought his fingers to his chin. "Well, would you mind if I had a drink, then? While I gather my bearings?"

"Course not, but your marks are no good here." Thomas sighed. "I could maybe work out a trade in exchange for any items you might have. Just can't use your notes."

"Oh, I have British coin."

Thomas put the rag in his apron and spread his hands as if to display the place's condition. "Don't have much, but——"

"Gin would be fine. Thank you."

"Plenty of that," Thomas remarked. "Some Boodles in the back." He sidled past Johan.

"Would you mind if I sat at your table, Mr. Dawls?" Johan asked. "I've had a long trip."

"Help yourself," Thomas mumbled, digging through a dark recess, his words congested.

Johan made his way to the table and hooked his cane over the back of a wicker chair. He sat down and removed his hat, relishing the soft breeze at his face. The snapping of a wood crate resounded from Thomas's direction as the man muttered to himself. Johan crossed his knee, taken in by the stillness of the land. He sighed as the warm wind leaked farther into the tent, fluttering the propped canvas and dragging grass and scraps of straw along the ground. It was as though the Karoo itself was breathing, inhaling every minuscule object, unable to refrain from touching even the tiniest bit of foreign particle.

"Here you are." Thomas put a half-empty bottle of Boodles on the table and produced the tin mug from his apron. He handed it to Johan.

"Thank you."

"Wee bit short, this one." Thomas rubbed his hands together. "Sometimes the boys at the platform sneak a few swigs before hammering the crates back up. You can always tell by the bruised wood at the corners."

"It's perfectly all right," Johan said, pouring the gin. "Mr. Dawls, I hate to bother you, but do you know where Karl's home might be? Or perhaps someone who could tell me his whereabouts? I really do need to find him."

Thomas's gaunt face grew pensive—a caricature of someone unable to discern between engaging or walking away.

"I'm an old friend of his," Johan offered, "really. He invited me down here to assist——" He cut himself off, remembering Karl's concern in the letter. *Suspicion is rampant here; be cautious of what you impart.*

"Yeah." Thomas exhaled. "Like I said, haven't seen Mr. Rynth in quite some time. Though to be honest with you, Doctor, it's a bit queer he'd invite you down here, what with everyone getting sick and all. Seein' as you're not here to help."

Johan took a sip of gin. "I see…well, unfortunately, I'm not that kind of doctor. Mr. Dawls, when was the last time you saw him? Karl, that is."

The young man looked up at the fluttering roof of his tent, thinking. "Couldn't have been this month. Heard he's been busy with something out there." Thomas pointed toward the Karoo. Johan followed the young man's finger to where a stream of thin clouds kicked at the foothills.

"Yeah, heard Mr. Rynth's been occupied with some project out there. Only heard rumors, so not sure what, but I might know a chap can maybe tell you. Adlai Courner. Sort of meet 'n' greet bloke for all those businessmen come after the war. Lots of good mining in the Orange and Transvaal."

Johan retrieved his pipe and leaned his elbows on the table. He was growing weary with Thomas.

"Where might I find this…Mr. Courner, then?"

Thomas parted his mouth. A trickle of snot ran down his nose.

"He frequents the pub. Has a private room where he likes to do his work. Otherwise, he's probably at Governor Tuner's, maybe about town running errands for him."

Johan packed the bowl of his pipe, pulled a match from his coat, struck its head against the table grain. "I see." He exhaled a thick cloud of smoke into the breeze, then took another sip of gin. "What's the name of this pub again?"

"Oh, the pub." Thomas drew the words out. "Don't really have a proper name, but most take to calling it the Croak and Grunt."

"Thank you, Mr. Dawls. I'll be sure to find my way there."

The sound of a toppled tin mug drew the men's attention. A pair of children had crept into the tent, snatching at what they could.

"Go on! Get out!" Thomas shooed at them with his crusty rag. Johan watched with an amused smile through the parted flaps of the tent as the dark children ran off toward the town's wall, their dyed garments flowing amid whirls of raucous laughter. Beyond them, a low whistle blew into the empty afternoon. As Thomas held the flaps of his tent open, glaring after the children, the train's groaning body could be heard bellowing over the tracks, headed back to De Aar. Johan swallowed the last of his gin and poured another glass from the bottle. The train was getting farther away, and its clatter diminished in a vacuum of sapphire sky as if it were a ship sinking to the depths of some unfathomed ocean.

Johan flared his nostrils and clasped his wrinkled hands together. There was something off—something uncomfortable—about this place. The town's very existence seemed crude, forced. He pulled his pipe from his mouth and clanked it over the table, dumping ash to the straw-covered floor.

"Mr. Dawls," he said, "can you call those children back in here? I have a job for them."

The avenue was empty, save for a roaming dog and an emaciated horse tethered beside a water basin. The storefronts creaked and tittered against the warm wind, cast in the shadow of early evening, their interconnected stoops a barren causeway of billowing dirt.

"This is it, ja?"

One of the children looked up at Johan. "Croak 'n' Grunt!"

Johan smirked and tapped his cane on the dirt, directing them to heave his trunk up the wooden steps to the dilapidated porch. He gave them an English shilling and watched as they ran off down the quiet avenue, their small shadows trailing in the setting sun. He grabbed his trunk and opened the shabby front door into a dim room full of tobacco smoke; a handful of men sat inside, each seated at least a table apart from one another, drinking in silence beneath a broken ceiling fan. Johan approached the bar, wary of the eyes that followed him. If he listened carefully, the cackled notes of some obscure symphony could be heard warbling from a backroom somewhere. He looked up at the bartender—a large black-haired man.

"Good evening," Johan said. "Would you happen to have cold beer? It's quite hot out."

The bartender looked Johan over with an amused air and turned to pour him a warm pint. "German, huh? What brings you?"

"I'm looking for Mr. Courner, actually. I was told he's a liaison for your town, that he might be able to help me."

"Another foreign business investor, hmm?" The bartender shook his head, ran his tongue over his teeth, set Johan's beer down on the bar. "Well, you're in luck. Adlai's in the back room there." He stuck his thumb out and pointed behind him to the brown door beside the shelves of liquor.

"Oh. Wunderbar. Would you mind telling him I'm a friend of Mr. Rynth's? I came a long way."

"I'm sure you did. He expecting you?"

"I should think someone is." Johan took a deep pull from his beer.

"Alright, alright," the bartender muttered, "just sit tight, and I'll see if I can't get him. There's a table over by the windows there. Help yourself."

"Thank you."

The bartender approached the brown door by the liquor shelves and gave it a series of gentle knocks. After a brief moment, the door opened to a crackling whine of violins and piano. Johan went to the empty table by the front windows as the bartender disappeared; he could feel the eyes of the other men resting on him, crawling over his suit. Johan took another gulp of beer. Through the Croak and Grunt's windows, he noted a peculiar absence of power-lines—the town was without electricity. The small shops across the way sat dark and foreboding, with only a few hanging lanterns to light their porches.

A man coughed at one of the tables behind him, then again, louder, hacking. Someone whispered for him to be quiet as the brown door behind the bar swung open. The bartender emerged, followed by a soft etude. He scoured the room, a look of intense scrutiny furrowing his thick brow.

"Alright, which of you has it?" His voice boomed clear and authoritative. The room sat motionless, save the slow, hovering haze of gray cigar smoke rising to the dead ceiling fan.

"I won't ask again," the bartender said. "Everyone knows the rules."

The man coughed again. Johan turned around, noticing his wide-brimmed hat. He sat sunken in his chair with clasped, shaky hands.

"Jesus, David," the bartender whispered. "You know you have to go…"

The man's hat bobbed up and down, slow, resigned.

"Now nobody touch him!" the bartender yelled. "Just let him go on. Miles, tell Captain Rael we found David outside trying to come in. Prop the door open so that he doesn't touch it on his way out. Don't tell the captain that David was in here!"

Another man—Miles, Johan figured—hurried to the door and jammed a piece of wood under it, then rushed out into the avenue and disappeared into the pale blue of evening, out of sight.

"C'mon, David," the bartender said, pointing toward the door. "We'll have no trouble if you leave. Please."

David stood as his chair produced a loud, reverberant scrape across the wooden floor. He whimpered and stumbled past the other men, stopping at the open door. He turned and looked at Johan, the eyes in his head watery.

"David! Out! Now!" the bartender yelled. David hacked once more, then lumbered down the steps to the avenue. The men in the bar all hurried to the doorway.

"Yap, there he is. That's Captain Rael alright," Johan heard a man say. He craned his neck over their bent shoulders and saw a tall man dressed in the British military's retired crimson stride down the avenue, tailed by an animated Miles and three soldiers.

"Shite…Davey's gone for good then, isn't he? Captain's brought the City Guard with him."

The men shuffled for better views.

"Naw, doesn't mean a thing. Dr. Lasser will fix him up. Just a cough is all."

"Quit your shoving!"

Johan took another sip of his beer and watched the soldiers lead David down a dark side street. The man in the crimson coat stood still, then turned and motioned to the bartender standing on the porch, giving a knowing nod.

"Aye now! You don't think the captain's coming in?"

The men fled to their respective tables as Captain Rael walked off, his saber jouncing at his side. The bartender kicked the piece of wood out from under the front door and closed it with a bang. He surveyed the room and the men, stomped over to the table David had taken-up and plucked the glass in his rag, then returned to the bar and dropped the half-full glass into a receptacle.

"Oi! German!" the bartender growled. "Mr. Courner said he'll see you—just head on back through the door. Your trunk will be fine where it is. No one'll touch it."

Johan stood with his beer and adjusted his glasses before taking a last look at the dusky avenue. He walked through the room with his cane clacking on the wooden floor, sensing the collective gaze of the Croak and Grunt's patrons coalescing on him once again. Was it his slouched figure? Or perhaps his gait? He stopped at the brown door, eyed the bartender, and set his empty pint glass on the bar. He then twisted the doorknob with a creak; the smell of sweet tobacco smoke filled his nostrils as he stepped into a small room covered with tattered green wallpaper, its cramped dimensions lit by two large lanterns. A squat round table with flickering candles stood in the center, occupied by a stout man in a pearl-gray weskit, writing in a journal. Across from him, a tall African man in a tidy black suit leaned against a wall beside a battered phonograph, its trilling of Chopin somewhat strained. The stout man peered up at Johan, his chubby face outlined with a red Van Dyke.

"Shut the door and come in," he said. "I'm Adlai Courner. Please, have a seat."

Johan did as he was told and sat in the empty chair; they shook hands between the candles.

"Am I to hear you were friends with Karl Rynth?" Adlai asked.

Johan set his cane against the edge of the table. "Yes, I've known Karl since university. We were the class of fifty-eight."

"Mmm." Adlai turned to the man at the wall. "Zithembe, would you mind getting our friend..." He gestured to Johan with an upturned palm.

"My apologies," Johan said. "Dr. Johan Mannswell."

"Right." Adlai smiled. "Zithembe, would you mind getting Dr. Mannswell a gin?"

Zithembe pulled his hands out of his pockets and headed to a low bureau where a line of bottles and glasses sat on a white towel.

"I'm afraid we've no ice out here," Adlai said, looking at Johan.

"Oh, that's quite alright."

Adlai produced a gold case from his vest and popped it open, offering Johan a trim, black cigarette.

"No, thank you," Johan said, patting the pipe in his coat pocket.

"As you will." Adlai put one of the sleek cigarettes in his mouth and grabbed a lit candle off the table. Zithembe returned with Johan's drink and set it down; he walked back to his spot on the wall, resuming his watch over the dark avenue outside.

"So," Adlai said, closing his journal, "what can I do for you, Dr. Mannswell? What brings you to our small station-town in the middle of June? I have to say, I wasn't expecting another profiteer, and...I can't seem to recall if Karl ever...spoke of you."

Johan took a sip of his drink. "Ah," he said, licking his lips, "yes, well, I'm just trying to find him. A personal affair. He wanted me to visit, and I was merely surprised to find him missing from the platform when I arrived."

Adlai leaned back with a slight frown and closed his eyes, taking a long pull off his cigarette. He exhaled a heavy sigh and fidgeted his ringed fingers over the buttons of his vest.

"Dr. Mannswell," he said, "I'm sorry to have to be the first to inform you—Karl...he...you see, he passed away almost three weeks ago."

14

The room swelled. The wallpaper patterns seemed to reach out like a tattered net, pulsing as the flames in the lanterns licked at their glass encasings. It was all so vibrant, yet drab and still.

"What? I don't...I don't understand. How?" Johan reached into his coat, mindlessly touching Karl's letter.

"A cave-in, I'm afraid. One of the more peculiar hazards of life as a surveyor." Adlai stubbed out his cigarette in the porcelain ashtray beside his journal; he leaned forward.

"I'm sorry, Dr. Mannswell," he said. "Are you alright? I suppose there's no really preparing one for such news."

Johan put his hand to his temples and removed his glasses. He was adrift at sea—a sailor besieged by a series of storms so subtle, so swift, he could already feel the anchors of exhaustion and doubt pinning him to the ocean floor. He should have never come; he should have brought Hendrik. Johan inhaled, the surprise of Karl's death a whirling pinwheel in his mind. "With Sylvia now, are you?" he whispered.

"What's that?"

"Karl's things, his property," Johan said, his eyes cast to his shoes. "I believe I have legal standing to sort his affairs, now that I'm here?"

"Mr. Rynth's estate," Adlai murmured, a tone of haughty amusement dwindling behind his words. "Yes...well, I think I can have the governor drum up some paperwork. The certificate of death is under file just down the street. Of course, I could have it delivered to you first thing in the morning. You're staying at the Herberg, yes?"

"I've not had time to check the accommodations of your town." Johan sighed, feeling weary. "I expected to find Karl waiting for me at the station. I sent several telegrams to the post here, letting him know when I was due to arrive."

"I see..." Adlai tapped his ringed fingers on the table and pulled at his red goatee. "Why exactly did you come down here, again, Dr. Mannswell? I'm curious. You're not here on business, and Karl—Mr. Rynth—was only a perfunctory land surveyor for wells of water.

Why should he wish you to come all the way down here? You say the two of you were friends, but..."

"He sent a letter, Mr. Courner. Something about an unusual discovery in your Karoo."

Adlai grew stiff. "Really?"

"Yes, and he spoke of a feeling. A concern, rather. He was wary. Worried."

Adlai's brow lifted.

Johan finished off his gin. "I came down to assist him at his request, but—"

"Again, just out of curiosity," Adlai cut in, waving his hand at a fly, "do you happen to have the letter on you?"

Johan weighed Adlai's interest against the sagging envelope in his breast pocket. "No," Johan said. "His letter was addressed to the head of my society. I was dispatched only because of the long friendship he and I shared."

Adlai pinched another cigarette from his gold case. His shoulders sunk as he relaxed his rigid posture. "Zithembe," he said, "will you take Dr. Mannswell's luggage over to the Herberg? Tell Martha his board is to be charged to my account."

Johan looked to Zithembe. "Thank you," he said, "but it's really no trouble. I can—"

"Nonsense," Adlai said. "Nonsense. Don't be silly. You've had a long journey, I suspect, and you must be hungry. How about tonight you join me at the governor's? He and his wife are hosting their weekly dinner in, oh"—Adlai checked his pocket watch—"about two hours. It might do you good to hear what he has to say about Mr. Rynth regarding this...discovery of his. Did you and he dig together often? I've heard stories of his time in Thatta...quite dramatic."

Johan narrowed his eyes. Adlai appeared to know something about Karl's past associations. A cryptic mention of societies would have otherwise intrigued the interests of a man like him, or at least prompted a discussion. Instead, Johan was being invited into a higher sphere of influence.

Johan exhaled. "I supposed I should be a terrible guest were I to shirk dinner with your governor. Very well. I accept."

"Great! Then it's settled." Adlai smiled, holding out his empty glass. "Zithembe, may we get two more?"

Zithembe obliged, moving without noise from the wall.

"Mr. Courner," Johan said, clearing his throat. "Um, Karl's body…it was recovered, yes?"

Adlai pursed his mouth. "The body? Well, I…no, why no, I don't think it was."

"Oh. Well, I'd like very much to pay my respects. Perhaps I could help organize an excavation of the cave-in, or—"

"Dr. Mannswell," Adlai said, "I realize you're eager for answers, but please, one thing at a time. Join me for dinner tonight. I'm sure Governor Tuner will give you all the information you require. He may even wish to help you, though our resources are quite limited. Here now, let us toast to your dear friend."

Zithembe placed the men's drinks on the table, spilling a bit of gin over the lip of Adlai's glass.

Chapter Two

Johan stood outside the Croak and Grunt beneath the solitary glow of an oil lamp. He leaned into his cane, smelling dried grass on the wind. Karl was dead.

"Governor's home is about two kilometers south of here," Adlai said, coming down the porch. "But the path is fairly hewn back. Shouldn't take us long to reach." He produced a flask from his olive-green coat and took a swig. "Zithembe will be around with the oxen soon."

Johan stared at the bleak number of flickering lanterns along the avenue, their dull glares divorced by rows of dark housing and sharp, starlit angles.

"Mr. Courner. What happened here?"

"Ah." Adlai played with the cap of his flask. "Influenza, I'm afraid. Ran into a bad spot of it some months back. Most left in April. Rest just took your train out today. Town's being abandoned, you see. But, with the war being over, I suppose there's no real reason for its being here…" Adlai took another pull off his flask and gave a smacked sigh. "Ports out east are won." He flattened his coat out with his hands and pocketed the container, the rings on his fingers knocking together with a muted clink.

Johan turned from the drunk Englishman to the sound of encroaching hooves, where he saw a dim yellow circle appear on the dirt ahead of a dark alley. Two pale oxen emerged from around a corner with a black carriage in tow. Zithembe rode atop in a shallow bench seat, teetering as he brought the carriage to a stop before the Croak and Grunt.

"Off we go, Dr. Mannswell." Adlai mounted the metal steps protruding from under the carriage and folded back its canvas roof. "Zithembe? Do you mind helping our doctor friend?"

Zithembe hopped down and held Johan's elbow with a gentle hand, guiding him into the carriage. Johan settled opposite Adlai as Zithembe clicked the low door shut and returned to his bench seat, manning the reins with a soft snap. The oxen clomped down the avenue, guided by the weak lamp at Zithembe's side. As Adlai lit a cigarette, Johan watched the Croak and Grunt's lantern recede into the night, the dark homes and storefronts crowding together, not unlike particular boroughs of Berlin.

Zithembe led them out of the station-town, past a series of inky stoops. In the open, Johan turned to see torches of orange fire along the station-town's squat border. A solitary soldier stood guard beside a bell-post, watching them pass. Johan felt a pulse in his chest. How insignificant. How fragile and weak this place was compared to the swath of darkness spread before them. Johan thought of the remaining souls huddled behind that short, shoddy wall, their collective fears of the night staving off whatever small feuds they waged during the day. He turned and faced Adlai, leaving the sight of the town behind him.

Above, stars twinkled and shimmered in a cloudless sky swaddled with strokes of translucent dust. Johan inhaled. The air was rich with the dirt of a place as yet nonplussed by the meddling of western civilization; the scent of dry grass overcame him again. Here, in the cool of the night, riding with strangers, Johan understood the allure such a place as this would have had on Karl—a place of solitude, where no one need discover him. Absolute freedom held dear within open land. Confidence surrounded by leagues of anonymity. Karl had always sought parts of the world few men went to; those areas fewer men stayed.

Johan cleared his throat. "Where did Karl live?" he asked. "I believe I saw a row of houses scattered outside the wall of your station-town. What would be its eastern side, yes?"

"Mmm." Adlai sat up and removed the cigarette from his mouth. "No. Those were never utilized, unfortunately. Think it was in January we got word there would be an influx of demobilized soldiers headed back to the Cape Colony. We'd already put the Boers in their place a good while before then, you see, and the ministry felt it was time to bring her boys in." Adlai shook his head with a smirk. "Soldiers only stayed a night or two…waste of timber, really. No, the only one to keep a permanent residence in that row was Dr. Lasser, who I'm sure you'll meet tonight."

"I see." Johan rubbed his chin. "Where did Karl live, then? I admit I have trouble imagining he stayed in town."

Adlai made a noise—a sharp breath. He pulled his flask out. "He…had his own place. A little farther away than Governor Tuner preferred. But yes, Mr. Rynth did enjoy his privacy, that is true." Adlai took a swig and wiped his mouth with the back of his hand. He stared at Johan. "I suppose you'd like to see it, eh?"

"I would," Johan said. "If I'm to settle Karl's affairs, I'll need to go through his belongings and see what can be shipped to Berlin. There will be a great many people distraught to learn of his passing. And I'm sure his notes over the past few years could prove valuable to my society."

Adlai made a subtle reach for the opulent buttons of his pearl-gray weskit. He wiped at his jowls, suddenly looking very tired. "Well, Governor Tuner is an amiable man," he said. "I'm sure it'd be no trouble if you wished to settle into Mr. Rynth's for the duration of your stay."

Was this Adlai's way of wanting to know how long he would be here? Perhaps it was in his best interest to withhold that information for now. Truth be told, Johan had no idea how long he planned on staying—or really what he was doing, now that Karl was gone.

The oxen snorted as the path grew rougher. Johan peered over the side of the carriage, squinting ahead of the bobbing lamp. A modest mansion sat bright and solitary on a ridge in the black distance, boasting over the land. "Is that the governor's?"

"It is," Adlai said. "Governor Tuner was able to procure a pair of dynamos from a man in the Orange. He had them installed in the cellar."

Johan felt relief at the sight of electricity, despite its source. The only realistic way to keep such machines refitted for constant use out here would be a limitless supply of hands to man the cranks. He looked up at Zithembe in the bench seat. Just how many of those hands were willing? Johan turned back to Adlai. "Did you fight in the war here, Mr. Courner?"

Adlai shook his head. "No, my interests lay elsewhere. Though, of course, I support the Crown and her endeavors. Tell me, as an archaeologist, you must have seen some exotic places. Any interesting finds on your digs?"

"Oh, I'm afraid I've always been more of a bookkeeper," Johan said. "Kept me close to my family. Though I was always drawn to the physical aspects of the job. No, my son's the real field-man in the family. He's been helping Robert Koldewey on his excavation of Babylon these past three years. I'm very happy for him—it's quite the achievement."

"Indeed," Adlai said.

The carriage bounced as the oxen labored up a hill. The path gradually steadied out beneath them, and the carriage eased over the rise, coming to a light gravel drive. The governor's manse stood erect in the night, electric lights beaming through every window on both levels, illuminating the front and side lawns. As Zithembe pulled the carriage into the rounded drive before the wide porch, Johan noted a sunken balcony wrapped about the second story; a section of its railing had broken off. He adjusted his glasses. On either side of the small mansion rose tall, slanted trees, their dark leaves rustling in the wind—cottonwoods, by the look of them, unnatural to the region and expensive to maintain.

Zithembe pulled the carriage to a stop and dismounted the

driver's bench, his boots scattering gravel as he landed. He helped Johan down while Adlai hobbled out the other side.

"Zithembe," Adlai said, coming around the carriage, "would you mind seeing to the animals? I'll call on you after dinner. Come, Dr. Mannswell, I think you'll find our governor to be quite the host."

Johan steadied himself on his cane and held the lapel of his coat close to his throat. The wind was active on the ridge; in the distance, the station-town appeared as a vague outline in the night. Johan peered up at the stars then, their numbers and cold light filling him with a sense of dread and unease—insignificance.

"Dr. Mannswell," Adlai called, "are you coming?"

Johan crunched through the gravel and joined Adlai on the wide porch. A dirt-stained chandelier hung above their heads, twisting on an ugly black wire in the breeze as its bulbs flickered and dimmed. Adlai took the front door's knocker in his hand and pounded. Movement was heard beyond—someone walking on open floors. Adlai smirked at Johan as a silhouette appeared in the fogged pane of the front door. It opened to a middle-aged woman in a blue dress, with long brown hair fashioned in a ribbon behind her shoulders.

"Adlai," she said, enthused and slurring. "Oh, Adlai, you'll be so *happy* to hear we've roasted lamb and apricot tonight!" She smirked at him with a knowing light in her eyes, swaying slightly in the doorway. She lowered her voice to a whisper. "I know it's your favorite."

Adlai cleared his throat. "Mrs. Tuner," he said, "I should like to introduce you to Dr. Mannswell. He'll be dining with us tonight if that's no trouble. I know Sal should be very interested to meet him."

Mrs. Tuner tilted her chin and studied Johan with a squinted brow. "There's always room for another at our table."

Johan removed his hat and stepped into a large, well-lit anteroom.

"Let me take your coats," Mrs. Tuner said.

Johan smiled at her and pushed his glasses up. She avoided his eyes and diverted her attention to Adlai as he hung his olive coat on a rack by the front door.

"Is he in his office?" Adlai asked.

"He's meeting with Otto. Oh, would you tell them dinner is almost ready? And don't get carried away with the aperitifs, dear. We've a lot of food to eat, but each course is portioned." She cast a glance at Johan. "The help worked very hard to get everything right."

Adlai took Mrs. Tuner's hand and gave it a pat. "I assure you we will consume every morsel. This way, Dr. Mannswell."

Johan followed Adlai into the main chamber, noting a stairwell on their left leading to the second story. They took a right at a grandfather clock, moving into a hallway decorated with peach-toned wallpaper and small electric lamps that curled out of thin wood paneling. The hall ended at a closed door, and Adlai rapped the backs of his fingers against it. "Governor Tuner," he called, "we have a guest. A friend of Karl Rynth's." He opened the door and stepped aside, revealing a spacious room set to a maroon palette.

Behind a large oak desk sat a slender man reclined in a metal chair, facing a set of windows that looked out into the darkness. The metal chair squeaked as it swiveled around; the man spread his long fingers across his weighty desk and smiled.

"Well, come in, come in. Adlai, it's nice to see you." A look of silent restraint emerged on the man's long face as he followed Adlai's movements. He wore a gray cardigan, perhaps one shade brighter than his combed hair. Johan stepped in after Adlai and extended his hand. The slender man rose to meet his grip.

"Sal Tuner," he said, squeezing Johan's fingers, "humble governor of these parts. You are?"

"Dr. Johan Mannswell." Johan darted his gaze from the governor's spider-black eyes to the surface of his oak desk, littered about with papers and bottles of ink under the spectral hue of a green banker's lamp.

"Please," the governor said, "have a seat." He sunk back into his metal chair while Johan turned to find a lean man seated on a small couch adjacent to the door. He wore an officer's coat—the British's retired crimson—his left leg crossed over his right. Johan tightened his grip on his cane.

"Oh, yes." The governor sighed. "Let me introduce you. This is

Captain Rael, our head of security, though I doubt there will be much to secure after the bloody exit we saw today, eh?" Governor Tuner let out a chuckle.

Captain Rael gave Johan a shallow nod, choosing to remain on the couch. He was young and clean-shaven with dark cropped hair.

"We were just discussing an interesting idea," the governor said. "A rumor, really. Dr. Mannswell, have you heard of this? About Paul Kruger hiding a cache of gold before the war's end? Otto happens to think—"

"Governor," Adlai interrupted, shutting the door, "I beg your pardon, but Dr. Mannswell has traveled a long way, and…I had the burden earlier of informing him about Mr. Rynth's…accident. At the dig site. You remember."

"Oh my," the governor murmured, a flicker of consideration rippling across his brow. "Well, forgive me, Doctor. Would you like a drink? Otto, would you care for another? I'll have another. Adlai, would you be so kind as to get us all another?"

Adlai gave a soft snort, then walked past Johan to the governor's bar at the far wall, next to a potted fern.

Captain Rael leaned forward on the couch, rubbing his bare chin. "We rarely get visitors, Dr. Mannswell, and I usually know when we do, so…why don't I know of you?"

"You must forgive the captain," Adlai said from the bar. "He's made a career out of being suspicious."

"I understand," Johan said, his voice barely audible, raspy. He was tired, and the animus emanating from the seated captain not only kept him standing but feeling like an old fool. He flared his nostrils; he had to keep vigil. "I'm sorry for intruding, and I thank you for welcoming me into your home, Governor, I—"

"Dr. Mannswell was sent a letter," Adlai informed the room. He approached the governor's desk with a drink in each hand. "Mr. Rynth requested his help regarding his discovery out in the Karoo."

"Oh?" Governor Tuner leaned forward in his chair and steepled his hands before his face. "My, my, how interesting that is."

Adlai extended a cocktail. Johan grabbed it and swirled the dark contents.

"Yes," Johan said, subduing a light tickle in his throat. "Karl wanted my help regarding an archaeological find of his, though I can't imagine what it might be." He took a sip of the cocktail and ran his tongue over his teeth. The mixture was thick but candied and calming. Johan patted his brown vest for his pipe and tobacco but remembered they were in his coat hanging in the anteroom. He felt for Karl's letter then. Still safe in his breast pocket.

"If you don't mind my asking,"—Johan made his way to the empty chair beside Captain Rael, the pain in his bad leg overcoming his hesitation—"how long was Karl here, exactly? I know he was employed by your government to survey new settlements around the outset of your war, but how long was he here specifically?" Johan settled into the chair and crossed his knee, tilting his head up to the men.

"Well," Governor Tuner said, "Mr. Rynth, as far as I can recall, was employed sometime in ninety-eight to scout around the Orange for potentially advantageous settlements, yes. And I believe he settled on this area while making his way back to Kimberly some time about a year later…why, you might even say Karl Rynth was the founding father of our little town." The governor chuckled to himself as his green banker's lamp briefly dimmed.

"I see." Johan took another sip of the syrupy cocktail. "Mr. Courner informed me that Karl had a house on the outskirts of your station-town. As I have the unhappy business of settling his affairs, I wondered if I might be able to stay there for a few days while I go through his belongings. He was a dear friend of mine, and…"

"Of course. Absolutely, of course. I'll have the key to Mr. Rynth's for you after dinner. Please, stay as long as you like." The governor pulled up a piece of paper and dipped his pen into a bottle of ink; its gold iridium point hovered over the parchment. "In fact… oh, let's see here…yes, let's have Mr. Rynth's belongings and estate put to your care and the key to his house in your possession. Oh! And let's get you some food and sundries. Get you settled right." The governor looked at Captain Rael. "Otto, do we still have Mr. Rynth's horse in the stables?"

Captain Rael lifted a dark eyebrow. "Last I checked."

"Perfect!" The governor put his pen back in its wood holster and raised the sheet of paper off the desk between two pinched fingers. He waved it back and forth with a slow, sweeping motion.

"Dr. Mannswell, I know you've seen the state of our town, and while I don't wish to alarm you, I feel it my duty to inform you that we've had a bit of an epidemic on our hands these past few months. Adlai would you…" He put the paper down on his desk, folded it with a gentle push, and then held it out. "So, you see, it might be better if you were to avoid the town as much as possible during your stay. Don't misunderstand me. We have things under control, but just in case, it might be better if you were to stay at Mr. Rynth's."

"Would you like me to see to these matters after dinner?" Adlai asked, holding the sheet of paper.

"What? Oh no, in the morning. Dr. Mannswell, are you staying at the Herberg this evening?"

"I am. Mr. Courner was kind enough to arrange my lodging."

"Ah, that's very good."

"How long will you be staying?" Captain Rael asked.

"I'm not at all too sure just yet," Johan said, turning to the young captain. "I had planned on several weeks under the impression Karl and I would be working on his find."

Captain Rael gave a subtle hum under his breath. Johan thought he detected an air of caged menace, but perhaps it was just the daft energies of a young man with nowhere to go. The captain put his hands on his knees and leaned closer to Johan. "Are we to believe Karl told you nothing of what he was working on out there?" His voice lowered. "Dr. Mannswell. Really. How cockeyed do you think we are?"

A knock came at the door; Mrs. Tuner emerged in her blue dress.

"Dinner is ready, gentlemen," she declared, then in a mocking tone, she added, "I know you are all up to important, secret business, but I for one am famished! Also, Dr. Lasser has arrived and said he——" She looked down at Johan in the chair, holding the syrupy cocktail.

"Oh, dear," she said. "I told you to watch the aperitifs! Adlai, how could you? The man probably hasn't eaten all day! He'll be starving by now!"

Johan sipped his drink, noting the glance Governor Tuner gave Adlai, who subsequently left the room, muttering an apology to Mrs. Tuner.

❧

Johan put his hand to his forehead, shielding his eyes from the dining room lights. He shifted in his chair and pulled his arms closer to his body. Somehow, despite the table being rather long for the room, his position between Adlai and Dr. Lasser was a claustrophobic one. He had been surprised by the town doctor; the man was maybe barely into his twenties, and despite a heavy English accent, it was clear he originated abroad—his dark complexion all but secured that fact. Johan peered past Captain Rael and Mrs. Tuner to the yellow walls of the dining room. Framed daguerreotypes of limp lions beneath proud hunters hung as decoration— perhaps commemoration. He scoffed to himself. It was so naturally British—the need to surround oneself with constant reminders of conquest. He sighed and lowered his hand to the white dinner cloth as Governor Tuner came to sit at the head of the table, smoothing out ruffles in his gray cardigan. He offered Johan a wink and rang an old dinner bell that rested by his plate.

At the sound of a swinging service door, Johan turned his head. A young woman emerged with a bottle of wine. His blood slowed to a crawl—it was uncanny, the resemblance almost wicked.

"This is Edith," Governor Tuner said. "She's new. And doing quite well here, I should add."

Johan rubbed his eyes. It had to be the long day. He was tired, but it could not be contested. The young woman's likeness to Sylvia was too absolute, even down to the style of her hair, save its yellow hue. Yes, he was positive; were this girl to have the same mousebrown hair, she could have passed for his wife on the day they met! And yet, beyond this—beyond his confusion at the young woman's likeness—it was in the way her shadow seemed to linger behind her body that disturbed him, as though taking its time relishing the darkness it cast over the walls and plates and pictures. He pulled at his cuffs and tried setting his attention on Governor Tuner as Edith went around filling the glasses.

"So, before we begin," Governor Tuner said, "I'd like to make a welcoming toast in honor of our new German friend, Dr. Mannswell. While it is unfortunate we should be made to meet under the tragic circumstance of Mr. Rynth's passing, let it not go unsaid that providence is a painful curriculum, but also rather a blessed one. One which has endowed us all here with the good doctor's presence." The governor took a sip of his wine.

Johan glanced around at the others, setting his glass down a bit too hard on the table. A claret ripple lipped over the crystal brim. He rubbed his thumb over the glass's bleeding stem before it reached the white table cloth, then followed Edith with the corners of his eyes as she made her way out of the room. Yes, her blond hair was just like Sylvia's—pulled back in a neat, short cut. Granted, her stride was all wrong and far too stiff. She was much taller, as well. Johan pursed his lips then, wondering why the feminine styles of Germany almost forty years ago should have a hold on the young woman.

"Dr. Mannswell." Dr. Lasser turned to him. "What brought you to study archaeology? If you don't mind my asking."

Johan shifted in his chair. He attempted a courteous tone and hoped the young man found him amicable.

"I suppose I always had a fascination with things considered forgotten or rubbed over." Johan picked up his wine glass. "Mankind is illiterate when it comes to its history"—he took a sip—"and its mistakes."

Dr. Lasser assented. "Where did you study?"

"Heidelberg."

"Ah, I'm an Oxford man, myself, though I'll admit it took a bit of finagling on the part of my brother-in-law to get me in. Really, he was more of a father to me."

Johan pursed his lips. "Not to pry, but—"

"It's perfectly alright. I'm used to it." Dr. Lasser wiped a smear of wine from his mouth with a napkin. "My older sister caught the eye of a lieutenant colonel during one of his trips to Ceylon, and, though young as she was at the time, had foresight enough to agree to his proposal under the condition I come live with them in England. He was an incredibly strange man, I came to realize, but well-liked and well-to-do. Needless to say, there were no ether-frolics with my peers. Once I was accepted to university, I had to stay focused. Sharp." The young doctor stared at the ceiling lights.

"Well, your brother-in-law sounds like an understanding man," Johan said, looking for Edith.

Mrs. Tuner laughed at a joke the governor made, then tapped her wine glass with a thin spoon. A different girl entered through the service door, pushing a cart in front of her. Johan swallowed his disappointment.

The girl placed a porcelain bowl of soup beside his glass of wine. He squinted at the young woman with a gentle smile.

"So…" Mrs. Tuner beamed at Captain Rael. "Otto, *I* heard there was some trouble in town this evening. What happened? Oh, do tell us."

Captain Rael wiped his mouth. "Mmm, yes, well, it seems a man was sick in the Croak and Grunt. Didn't report himself."

"I was there. The man went by David, ja?"

The captain stared at Johan, then gave a smirk in Adlai's direction. "I believe that is the man's name, yes."

"What will happen to him?" Johan stirred the soup with his spoon. "I saw him being escorted away by a group of soldiers."

"David is in my care now." Dr. Lasser spoke up. "He's being seen to by my nurse. There's no need to worry. City Guard knows what it's doing."

"Well, I think it's just awful," Mrs. Tuner said. "That poor man being too afraid to mention he's sick with a cold."

"Dr. Mannswell," Captain Rael spoke low, chewing his salad, his blue eyes sunken and dark, "Adlai here tells me you're part of the DOG, is that true?"

"Ooh, what's…the DOG?" Mrs. Tuner whispered.

Dr. Lasser spoke to Mrs. Tuner across the table. "It's a private group in Germany, I think, associated with the archaeological study of Biblical sites." He turned to Johan. "Right, Dr. Mannswell?"

Johan took a sip of the broth. "Somewhat," he said, "though there is admittedly more to it than that. Der Deutsche Orient-Gesellschaft is involved in many things."

"Ooh, what does that mean?" Mrs. Tuner held her glass to her bosom.

"It's the German Oriental Society, my dear." Johan smiled at her.

"Well," Captain Rael continued, "regardless of its interests, Dr. Mannswell, I can only be led to wonder if whether or not Mr. Rynth was a part of your DOG as well."

Johan held the captain's gaze. "He was not."

Adlai cleared his throat. "Perhaps what the captain here is trying to get at is if we should be expecting any more…emissaries…from your society."

Governor Tuner made a noise of agreement through a mouth full of wine.

"Would that raise issue?" Johan asked.

"Oh no," Adlai said, "not issue, just…if it's a possibility, I should think we'd like to prepare for it…in the event that your people come."

"Our concern is strictly from a timed, economic standpoint," the governor muttered. "You see, our station-town is to be abandoned within the next few months."

Dr. Lasser laughed nervously. "They've already taken down the telegraph lines."

"Yes." Governor Tuner eyed the young doctor. "Yes, but the people I'm sure you saw as you arrived, Dr. Mannswell, were our last real residents. And the train won't be coming back until next week. Afterward, it'll be set to arrive once a month until December, when we leave on its final trek to the Cape."

"We have plenty of bodies to see that things function fine until then," Captain Rael said, "but if your German friends decide to follow you and begin grubbing for Mr. Rynth's little project out here in the Karoo, there might not be any of us here to help out with the Bushmen. And make no mistake, fierce they are."

"I see." Johan wiped his lips and placed his napkin on the table. "Well, let me assure you, my society's interests will be of no hindrance. Governor, gentlemen, lady Tuner, I've had a long day. One of great loss. As of now, I wish only to see to Karl's affairs. If there's time in the interim before the next scheduled train, perhaps I might request a guide take me to his final resting place."

"If there's time?" Dr. Lasser looked incredulous. "Sir, were I to come across such a revelation equivalent to the realm of medicine, I'd be beside myself with—"

"Samith!" Adlai shook the table, visibly angry at the young doctor.

Mrs. Tuner finished her glass of wine and tapped it with her dinner fork. Her face fell into a sallow, displeased version of itself as the young girl from earlier scurried into the room with her cart and a bottle of Grand Constance. She cleared the half-eaten soup and refilled everyone's drinks.

"Karl never told me what he found," Johan said, speaking to Dr. Lasser, his eyes focused on the servant door, hopeful Edith would make an appearance. "And while I am interested in what my friend worked on before his death, I have no intention of discussing it during Mrs. Tuner's dinner."

"My, my." Captain Rael leered at Dr. Lasser, handing his glass to the servant girl. Dr. Lasser sank into his chair.

Adlai looked at Johan, then the governor. "Whole thing's collapsed anyway."

"Yes!" The governor almost laughed. "Yes, very unfortunate. Mr. Rynth was lost to us. The whole endeavor was lost to us."

Johan's brow furrowed. "Well, it must have been quite the excavation if Karl's site was deep enough to buckle in on itself. I should still like to see it, of course. If that's no trouble."

Governor Tuner cleared his throat and glanced at Johan, his spider-black eyes appraising him. "Adlai," he said, turning his gaze, "we'll need to transplant my wife's perennials back to our estate on the Cape before August's end. Can you have plans drawn up by July?"

The servant girl emerged with Mrs. Tuner's second course, a large pot of stew. The odor was heavy with potatoes and carrots; Johan's mouth began to water.

"Dr. Mannswell," Mrs. Tuner said, attempting her prior light mood, "I'm dying for you to try this. I believe they call it…potjiekos. We're trying something new tonight. Something of a local favorite." She leaned over the table and fixed him a shallow bowl. Johan reached out, reminding himself that he would need to wait for the others before feeding himself.

"I do wonder," the governor said, blowing on his spoon, "how the Foreign Office plans to keep the Boers from causing another uproar this time. It's already happened twice now."

"I don't think that will be a problem." Captain Rael took his eyes off Mrs. Tuner and looked at her husband, his voice despondent. "Their numbers have always been smaller than ours, and after seeing what our sweeper groups did to them, I'd wager they'll stay in place this time."

"I suppose…" Governor Tuner appeared in thought. "What do you think, Dr. Mannswell? How about your country? Is the western reach of Africa having issue?"

Johan put his spoon down and wiped his mouth. He took a gulp of wine and swilled it around his tongue. "I don't think…" He cleared his throat. "I don't believe I have enough understanding of colonial politics these days to really say."

Mrs. Tuner interjected. "Sal, please."

"The dish is wonderful, Mrs. Tuner," Dr. Lasser said, his left leg jumping under the table with a nervous tic. His vulnerability reminded Johan of Hendrik, or rather Hendrik's lack thereof. He felt a twinge of pride and homesickness for his stoic boy.

Mrs. Tuner beamed. "Well, isn't that sweet."

"After dinner," Governor Tuner said, "I'd like it if you joined us upstairs in my study, Dr. Mannswell. Purely a ritual I like to employ upon all my guests."

"Of course." Johan paused. "Though I'd like to gather my pipe from the anteroom if that's alright."

"Absolutely, it's alright! A cigar and some port sounds most fitting indeed! Don't you agree, Otto?"

The captain chewed at a chunk of game from his stew. "As good a way to end the evening as always, Governor."

Johan noted Adlai had barely touched his bowl of stew and that Dr. Lasser was becoming more remote, sulking in quiet. Later, when the platter of roasted lamb and apricot sauce came to the table, the only banter was that of a trivial discussion between Governor Tuner and Captain Rael concerning rumors of Paul Kruger's cached gold.

Johan stood at the grandfather clock in the main hall and set his pocket watch to the time—just past nine. He ran his palm over his face. How was it possible? Could it be that Sylvia had come back to him? The very notion of Edith's lithe body stepping through the manor was an excess of emotion, the knowledge of her existence an itch on his heart. Was it even feasible for Edith to understand just how well he knew the personality of her figure, the conversation of her face, the subtle remarks of her form? That he could pinpoint when the dimples at her eyes would signal the arrival of a pouty smile? He watched the pendulum swing behind the clock's glass encasing, lost in thought.

The muted sound of splashing water came from behind a closed door down the hallway. Dr. Lasser emerged from the washroom, looking noticeably refreshed as he rubbed the crook of his right arm. Johan regarded the young man out of the corner of his eye.

"Oh, hello, Dr. Mannswell. Quite a dinner."

Johan nodded, putting his watch away. "Adlai mentioned the governor hosted weekly. Are they always like this?"

"Each Saturday." Dr. Lasser smiled. "But no, they usually don't have anything to do with archaeology and unusual finds. I can tell Sal was surprised by you. We all were, Dr. Mannswell." The young doctor lowered his voice to a whisper. "I need you to listen. It's about what Karl found out there. They wish to keep it secret. You must come to me when you can—"

"Samith." Adlai came through the dining room, wiping his brow with his kerchief. "Are we still on for lunch tomorrow? Dr. Mannswell, would you like to join us?"

Johan pushed his tongue against his cheek, annoyed at the Englishman's timing. "Perhaps another time, Mr. Courner. I should like to get to work on the papers concerning Karl's estate. I'm to be escorted to his home, yes?"

"Why, of course." Adlai smirked. "Zithembe and I will pick you up at the Herberg around ten in the morning. We'll see to it you have all you need while you're out there."

"It's really not that far from town," Dr. Lasser offered. "You could walk...if you ever had to."

Johan rapped his cane against his bad leg. "Not with this," he said, then turned to Adlai. "Was I correct in hearing Karl had a horse? I'm to receive the beast as well?"

Adlai appeared short of breath. "Yes."

Governor Tuner entered the main hall with Captain Rael then, the two of them sharing a laugh. "Ah, wonderful," the governor said. "You're all here. Oh, Dr. Lasser, thank you for coming. Same time next week?"

Johan lifted an eyebrow; this was curious. Why would Dr. Lasser be removed from Governor Tuner's ritualistic digestif?

"Thank you for the pleasant meal," Dr. Lasser murmured, his lips set together. "I'll...see my way out. Please tell Mrs. Tuner I had a wonderful evening, as always." He looked to Johan and extended a hand. "It was a great privilege to meet you, Dr. Mannswell. I hope we have an opportunity to chat more in the coming days."

Johan took the doctor's hand; the man was nervous, his brown eyes connecting with Johan's, relaying discretion. Johan withdrew from the handshake.

"Ready for port, are we?" The governor chuckled. "Ah! Dr. Mannswell, did you retrieve your pipe like you wanted?"

"I did, thank you."

"Splendid. This way, then. Good night, Samith!" Governor

Tuner mounted the stairs with Captain Rael in tow. Johan looked to Adlai, the man's corpulent arm dramatically outstretched toward the staircase.

"After you," he said.

Johan obliged and grabbed the banister, careful with the amount of weight he gave to his cane. He took a step and immediately winced.

"Would you like some help?"

"No, Mr. Courner. I can manage."

At the top of the stairs, Johan found the second story sprawled in darkness—how grateful the servants in the cellar must be, resting beside their dynamos now that the governor's ego was satiated, his need to illuminate every fixture in the house quelled for the moment.

"Down that way, Dr. Mannswell."

Johan turned to his left, spotting an open doorway at the end of a long hall. The room beyond bled weak lamplight onto a varnished wood floor. He walked toward the glistening orange sheen, his cane's loud tapping accompanied by a low chuckle that eased out of the encroaching doorway, as though the room itself found Johan's approach foolish and asinine. It was the governor, laughing at a remark he told the captain, and however jocular the joke, it was also clearly private, for as Johan entered the study, their stony faces glared at him. Johan cleared his throat and looked around.

The study was spacious and well-kempt, with large potted plants and dark red walls. The glass panels of the windows had been thrown open to the night, and on either side of the room sat small leather sofas accompanied by a beige rug set in the middle of the floor, its ends curled just before a soft honey-colored armchair. Johan paused at the governor's writing desk, his attention overtaken by the only painting in the room. It filled the entire wall, depicting an emerald river running through dark forested hills that coiled to a murky lake beneath dull, bluing clouds—utterly entrancing. Johan adjusted his glasses. The vantage was from up high, presumably off the peak of a taller hill—such longing, such visceral nostalgia for a place he had never been.

"Beautiful piece, isn't it?" The governor sidled up with two drinks in his hand, offering one to Johan.

Johan took the glass without thinking. "What is it?"

Governor Tuner chuckled. "Teal Annayr. Somewhat of a mystical place from an era long ago, I'm told. Purely fictitious, of course…"

"Governor," Adlai called as he shut the door to the study, "shall we go ahead and get settled? Dr. Mannswell and I still have a long ride ahead of us."

"Ah, yes, right, right." The governor held Johan's gaze for a moment, then extended his hand. "Before I forget. The key to Mr. Rynth's home." Governor Tuner clapped Johan on the back, then left him for a seat on the empty sofa across Adlai and Captain Rael.

Johan found himself alone. He put Karl's key in his vest and went to the honey-colored chair. As he sank into the cushions, he wondered—had he been manipulated to take this seat? The painting was in full view, its borders looming at the edges of the ceiling and walls. He gave a sigh and put his glass of port on the small side table next to his chair, then anxiously loaded his pipe as he waited for one of the men to speak. The silence of Governor Tuner's after-dinner ritual felt overtly business-like in nature.

Captain Rael rolled the ashen tip of his cigar over a bronze ashtray set in the arm of the sofa, then leaned forward and hiked his slacks up, brushing the tapered end of his crimson coat behind his thigh. "Dr. Mannswell," he said, "about your German friends… your society having no immediate plans of coming down to investigate Mr. Rynth's work…well, I've given it some thought. Tell me. Your being here is an official position, is it not? And as such, don't you think the matter of an international emissary might have gone through our regional Foreign Office? In a sense, shouldn't we have known of your impending arrival?"

Johan sighed and sipped at his port.

"Captain, please." Governor Tuner put his palm out. "Really now, you're making a terrible impression on our guest. So hard you are, Otto. Dr. Mannswell has traveled a long way. He merely wants to see to Mr. Rynth's property, yes? There's no backchannel of espionage here. Clearly. Why good God, Adlai just informed him of his colleague's death mere hours ago. I say Dr. Mannswell and his society can have all the range they desire. Who cares? We'll be gone from here soon enough."

Johan struck a match with his fingernail and dipped it into the bowl of his pipe. Did the river in the painting move? He squinted as he fluttered the flame out. The strokes of paint bordering the canvas were like the edges of a window, and inside lay a sprawling, unreal landscape of sad beauty and wonder.

"Now I know our two countries have had some conflict," Governor Tuner continued, "but a man's nation does not think for him."

"I've taken no offense," Johan said. "As every God demands fidelity, so do the rulers of nationalities, it would seem. Although, I do wonder if the young captain here is aware of his name's origin? It's really quite common in Germany." Johan took a pull at his pipe. Captain Rael sat back, giving his bruise-blue eyes a roll as he smirked.

The governor cleared his throat and clapped his hands together as if trying to banish harmful air from the room. "Right! Well, shall we get to the matter of Mr. Rynth's discovery? Bring Dr. Mannswell up to speed, as they say?" He patted the pockets of his cardigan and produced a large, garish pipe. "Adlai," he said between clenched teeth, "would you be so kind as to inform Dr. Mannswell of the events concerning, ah, the collapse of Mr. Rynth's dig? Maybe a timeline?"

Adlai's face hung open. He set down his glass of port and leaned forward, blocking Johan's view of the captain as he pulled at the ends of his red Van Dyke. "Well, roughly a month ago," he said, his voice weak, "Mr. Rynth was furthering excavations of the area he had been working on since late winter. There was a small structure he built above it. A way to lower men down."

"Are you saying what he found was never exposed?" Johan cocked an eyebrow.

"Ah…" Adlai faltered. "I don't…I don't believe it was exposed beforehand, no."

Johan puffed at his smoldering pipe. "Surely, some sign led Karl to investigate the area. A depression in the soil perhaps…"

"Dr. Mannswell." Adlai sighed. "I'm not as knowledgeable as Mr. Rynth or yourself in these matters. We're not entirely sure what happened, only that last month the ground gave way, and several men lost their lives. Including Mr. Rynth."

"I see." Johan rubbed his chin. "Would any of you gentlemen happen to know when Karl came across this site of his?"

"It was luck," Captain Rael said, his voice carrying the tone of someone bored, recalling a trite event far away in his memory; he had become mellow and laconic with port. "Karl and I went hunting for big game last January." The captain waved his hand. "That's when we came to it."

Adlai took a sip from his glass, looking at the captain. He flicked the ash from his black cigarette and leaned back, dabbing at his forehead with his kerchief.

Johan peered at Captain Rael. "What did the two of you find, Captain?" He took a pull off his pipe and darted a glance at the governor. The man seemed pleased with himself, his face set in a sardonic grin.

Captain Rael swirled his glass. His voice was tense, manicured. "Well, we were only some hours out of town with ample supplies and hoped to be back the following Friday with a trophy or two…" He gave a strained smirk. "We came off a hill and spotted a group of mokalas clustered in the distance. Something of a shaded haven, really. A rarity in these parts." The captain stared at his glass of port. "So, we started out for the group of trees—this grove. And there, in the middle, a clearing of grass." Captain Rael flashed a bizarre grin at Johan. "And the center of the clearing? A hole in the ground."

"A rather large hole," the governor said, his smile widening as he reclined on his sofa, garish pipe in hand.

"Yes," Captain Rael continued, his blue eyes leering at nothing in particular. His slick face was pale in the candlelight, as though cast from wax. He lowered his voice to a mumble. "Only…it was…uprooted. Outward-like…like something dug its way up and——" There was a moment of silence as he cut himself off.

Johan uncrossed his bad leg and reached for his port. "I'm sorry," he said, "forgive me, but do you mean to say something dug itself out of the ground?"

"No, no." Governor Tuner laughed, injecting levity into the room. "No, that's not what Otto meant. He's just saying it *looked* like something dug its way out of the ground. Really now, Captain, don't be absurd. Dr. Mannswell, the hills of this region are remarkable structures of nature, formed in some of the most abstract of designs. It's well known the Karoo can have…effects on not just what people see but…their imaginations as well."

Captain Rael sat back, his complexion waning as whatever blood pumped through his body drained from his face. "Port's gone to my head," he said.

Johan took his pipe from his mouth and exhaled a plume of smoke. "Did the two of you investigate further? What did you see?"

Captain Rael peered at the governor. "Nothing. Couldn't make-out a thing. It was dark…like a well."

"And?"

"And so I persuaded Mr. Rynth to mark it up on his map for a later expedition once we inquired with the governor here," Captain Rael finished, his tone curt. He then nodded to himself and plucked his stubby cigar from its angle on the ashtray.

The men sat in quiet, listening to the wind brush against the manor as it lightly throttled the open windows and rustled the governor's drapes. Johan ran his palm along his face, wanting to feel youth there, to feel vigor and hope; instead, there was a weakness, frailty of loss. He waited, expecting the governor or Adlai to add to the captain's account. But they remained silent, and he felt small in the broad chair. Johan finished his drink and set the glass down. He looked at Governor Tuner. "So, what did Karl say?"

"Mmm? About what?" Governor Tuner smiled.

"About the hole that he and the captain found. What did he say to you?"

The governor puffed at his large pipe, then stood and grabbed a crystal of bourbon off his bar. "I'm feeling a stronger nightcap is in order before we part." He walked over to Captain Rael and Adlai, pouring a splash for each. The governor approached Johan and filled his empty glass to the brim. "Mr. Rynth came to me later that same day with Otto," he said. "He told me what you just heard. So I told Mr. Rynth we would work out a labor arrangement with a few of Otto's men, do as he wished. The area was far enough away and therefore guaranteed no intrusion into our business affairs. Quite frankly, that's about the last I heard of it...until the unfortunate collapse a month ago."

"Ah," Johan said, realizing he had no power to take this any further, "I suppose that sums the matter up for now. Thank you, gentlemen. I shall include these conversations in my report and inform my society once I reach a proper line. You say the train should be arriving in a week?"

"Yes," Adlai said, "and, of course, you'll have all the courtesy we can provide throughout the duration of your stay."

Johan raised his glass of bourbon, and the others lifted theirs in response. An air of mutual unease emanated off each man until it seemed to fill the study and vacate through the open windows, floating off into the warm night. Johan peered over the rim of his glass, watching the painting of Teal Annayr across from him, how the dark lake swelled as the minor shades of setting sun diminished behind forested hills—hills he swore held a brighter pigment not ten minutes ago.

Chapter Three

MORNING ROUSED HIM OUT OF A DEEP SLUMBER, ITS BRIGHT tendrils sifting through the room's slatted window, lacerating his eyes. Johan tussled in the stiff sheets, turning from the sun. He was groggy, parched, and congested. Naked and frail, he sat up and reached for his cane by the nightstand. Johan stood and shambled over to the alcove by the wardrobe, where a small chamber pot had been left for him. His back clamped up as he relieved himself. Smacking his lips, he made his way back to the bed and sat atop the sheets; already, the room was growing hot.

Johan plucked his pocket watch from the nightstand and squinted. It was a little after seven in the morning. He laid back on the pillows and let the events of yesterday unfurl in his mind. Thinking of the dinner at Governor Tuner's, he remembered Dr. Lasser's ominous remark. Johan swung his legs over the bed, groaning as he bent down and rummaged through his scattered clothes. He picked up his vest and pulled out his pipe and tobacco, then sprinkled a dry hash into the bowl under a shaft of sunlight riven by floating particles. Staring at the wooden slats of the window as the golden morning filled the room, he grabbed a clay pitcher from the nightstand and poured a glass of tepid water, gulped it down, and finished making his pipe, striking a match off the wall.

The room was tiny, consisting of his bed, a wardrobe, and the alcove where his chamber pot had been placed; he noted his traveling trunk and blew a cloud of blue smoke toward the ceiling. Johan rose, narrowing his eyes with concern as his pipe dangled from his mouth. The lock on his trunk had been picked; someone had rummaged through his belongings.

He hobbled over, then knelt with some effort and flipped the pine lid open. Everything appeared in order, his clothes folded just as they were, neatly in place under the traveling straps, but the journal beneath his clothes had been removed and put back. It was at a completely different angle than he left it. Johan picked up his journal and found a wooden picture frame laid face down among his socks; with a shaky hand, he reached and turned it over.

"Mein Gott…"

It was a charcoal sketch of them—all three of them. Karl stood smug with his arm around Sylvia's waist, her delicate hand reaching up to his shoulder. Johan, rigid and shy beside her, clutched a stein of beer in both palms as he wore a look of uncertainty. They were standing before a bar with a large mirror behind them. Johan scooted against the frame of the bed and gave a low snort as that night returned to him. It was the night Sylvia had come into their lives; when Karl purposely bumped into her and spilled her drink. By the end of it, Karl had given an amateur artist from the university the last of his money for a sketch; the louse must have kept it ever since. Johan ran his fingers over the frame's glass pane. The parchment inside had yellowed over the years; most of Karl's right side was awash with ravenous mold now, and Johan's own left arm was nearly missing. Sylvia, however, remained whole, her grace and beauty forever caught between the pull of Johan and Karl's desire. Oh, how they had both vied for her affection that night! A sad smile crossed Johan's mouth as he studied her features then—the same as the servant girl's.

He sighed and let the picture sink to his lap. Zithembe had been the only person with access to both his luggage and room; what did it mean, him putting this here? Why would Zithembe have such a personal artifact of Karl's in the first place? Johan traced his thumb over Sylvia, rasping his fingers against the back of the frame. There was a bulge near the bottom right corner; something was packed behind the sketch. He laid the frame face down on the floor and removed his pen from his journal. Johan inserted its plated point into the frame's siding and leveraged up the wood panel. His heart thumped as he pulled out a piece of thick parchment with loose handwriting:

Under the floorboards beneath my desk.
Keep it on you.
-30.0007°, 24.4728°

The Herberg's lobby was spacious but empty, with several small tables covered in a fine layer of dust. The white plastered walls were sparsely decorated with displays of dried grasses crossed together like swords. A single lion head hung mounted above the double-doors leading outside to the avenue. Did such cats sneak into the homes of men, only to be trapped and killed before stealing away their prey? Johan sneered to himself—the English and their trophies.

He turned around at the base of the stairs and saw a shelf of mail slots littered with rags and odd tools that lined the far wall. Johan walked over and rolled up his yellow shirt sleeves as his brown slacks rasped in the quiet. He clacked his knuckles on the sanded surface of the counter, then adjusted the trim of his vest at the sound of someone rising off a chair in the backroom. A middle-aged woman emerged from around the nook. She had salt-white hair and a tired face—a face Johan knew well. A face awake with loss. He wondered who she buried: a child? A husband?

"You the guest up top?" she asked. "Mr. Courner's German doctor?"

"I am." Johan nodded.

"We already got a doctor. He isn't white, but he is British."

"Ah, well, I'm not a doctor of medicine."

The woman looked him over. "Guess you want breakfast. We got eggs, few potatoes. And I make my coffee stronger than most. I've only a little milk left in the pale. You're welcome to it."

"If it's no trouble."

The woman stared at him with a furled eyebrow.

Johan gave her a weak smile, tugging at the roll of his sleeve. She pursed her mouth and walked back to the nook under the stairs, shaking her head. Johan sighed and headed for a table by a window. He took a seat and peered through the curtains into the sunny avenue. Hot dust billowed over the ground, snapping at the ankles of a few scattered people going about their early chores. They moved as if crossing below the sun were a risky maneuver, each of them bound for the shade of a porch.

He checked his pocket watch; it was now a little past eight, but the faint smell of fresh coffee hit him. For a moment, his concerns were put aside. The woman approached his table and placed a large steaming mug before him, followed by a small decanter of questionable milk.

"Eggs'll be ready soon as I tender the potatoes."

"Thank you."

The woman walked off as he poured a dollop of milk and stirred it with a spoon. He took a sip; the brew was potent. At the sound of clopping hooves, he looked again to the avenue. A black horse was being led by a soldier. The man's uniform was dirty, his rifle bouncing at his back as flashes of sunlight glared off its bayonet. What did the soldier's daily regiment consist of, considering the British had won and the land they wanted lay far east of here? Johan took another sip of coffee. He supposed it was just the British way to keep an appearance of force.

The eggs and potatoes came, and by nine thirty-eight, Johan sat with his pipe, occupied with the goings-on of the avenue. The woman had taken his plate and mug and retrieved his trunk and hat from the upstairs room. "Under the floorboards beneath my

44

desk..." Johan mumbled to himself through the bit of his pipe. "Keep it on you..."

He heard a carriage pull up outside the Herberg's double-doors and turned to see the lion head mounted above, yelling in a muted cry. The doors opened, and the big cat's combed mane blew with the moving air of a hot day. It was Zithembe, dressed in his all-black suit. Adlai entered behind him, wearing a bowler hat and a long mauve duster. He removed his gloves and strode toward Johan as Zithembe shut the doors.

"Good morning, Dr. Mannswell. I see you managed to find some breakfast. Martha is known for her ham and eggs. How'd you like it?"

Johan puffed at his pipe in a grimace. The damnable woman had ham the whole time. "Wunderbar..."

"Excellent. Well, shall we get going?" Adlai checked his watch. "Zithembe and I have a luncheon set with Samith, and it will take us about an hour to get you to Mr. Rynth's, which means another hour for us to return. We have groceries and oil for your lamps in the buggy's rear, and a heap of wood-chips for the stove."

Johan nodded and took a last look out the window, sniffling through his clogged nose. He could see strengthening thermals atop the buildings down the avenue. Today would be hotter than yesterday.

❧

"Water?"

Adlai's head bounced in the carriage as beads of sweat slowly made their way down his bloated, pink face. The canvas top had been folded up, allowing them a modicum of shade as they rode through the Karoo. Having opted to leave his coat in his trunk, Johan sat quietly, amused at the gaudy duster Adlai insisted on wearing.

"Well," Adlai said, rescinding his flask, "we were sure to pack you plenty of canisters. Karl dug a well if you happen to run low, though it may take a bit of pumping to get the reservoir up and flowing. No one's been out there for quite some time."

Johan studied the rocks passing by, the soft umber rolling out like a rug over the hills. "Does it ever get green out here?" he asked. "The renderings I've seen of Africa paint the continent much differently—much friendlier and greener."

"Mmm," Adlai grunted, fumbling with the top of his flask. "I don't know what to tell you. This region's semi-desert. Oh, that reminds me, you should probably rest Mr. Rynth's horse once we arrive."

Johan turned to see the old animal trailing behind them, its long, swinging tether wrapped through the luggage rack.

"It's an Andalusian," Johan said. "A beautiful creature. Its name?"

"Walter, I believe."

Johan smiled.

"Is that a funny name?" Adlai asked.

"No." Johan laughed, his throat sore. "Just…Walter's my middle name." He peered back at the animal, admiring the sheen of sunlight that glazed off its auburn coat.

Adlai took a swig of water. "You and Mr. Rynth were close," he said.

"We were, for many years." Johan's gaze drifted to a pair of mokalas crowning a knoll in the distance. "He had a gravity to him, you see. As if he had caught a glimpse of something greater, was touched by it, always pressed to search for it." Johan stared at Adlai. "Do you think he could have found it out here before he passed?"

Adlai wiped his mouth. "Men find many things out here, Doctor."

"Did you ever see it?"

"I'm sorry. See what?"

"Karl's excavation."

Adlai flared his nostrils and rolled his eyes. "No, Dr. Mannswell, I stay in town. There's nothing out here to interest me aside from the small fortunes men bring with them."

The carriage swayed as Zithembe led them along an incline.

46

"Captain Rael, he visited Karl often, yes?"

Adlai wiped at his brow. "No, no, Otto wasn't involved either. He just made sure Mr. Rynth had a soldier or two in case rogue Bushmen or bitter Boers came about. I believe Mr. Rynth found the captain's annual check-ups troublesome, though. He was a very solitary man."

"Yes, he was," Johan said. "Mr. Courner, last night the governor mentioned Karl worked out a labor deal with Captain Rael. I take that to mean his soldiers helped with the dig?"

Adlai answered in a low, drawn-out tone. "I believe so, yes…"

"Those men wouldn't be around, by chance, would they? I'd like very much to speak with them."

"I'm afraid they're all dead, Doctor. Either taken by the flu or lost in the site's collapse."

The two sat in silence, listening to the oxen and wheels. Zithembe clicked through his mouth, and the animals slowed to a stop. Adlai flashed a smile at Johan, then let a long sigh. "Appears we're here, Dr. Mannswell. You do have the key, I hope?" The stout man swung the carriage door open and hopped out, leaving Johan to wait for Zithembe's help. Johan pushed his hat on his head and grabbed his cane. When Zithembe lowered him down, he immediately picked up on the whiffle of a swirling barometer. He rounded the carriage and grinned at the sight of Karl's handiwork, the instrument having been hammered into an eave.

The house itself was small, painted a ruddy yellow and built on thick wooden supports. An outhouse stood several meters away near a rusted spout, and on the house's right sloped an open stable with a fluttering tin roof. Johan walked up the rise toward Adlai, and together, they climbed the warped steps to Karl's narrow porch. They stood in silence, listening as a weathered rocking chair bobbed back and forth in the breeze. An array of wind-chimes belled low and dull in the air, hung from a hook above the railing. Johan smeared dirt from a pane in the front window; a pair of tan curtains had been drawn against the sun. He then took Karl's key from his vest pocket and clicked back the bolt with a labored twist.

The home smelled of dry wood and kerosene yet felt cold and

dark. The main room was bare aside from a plaid couch and an empty bookshelf; the jade rug in the middle of the floor was more like a tattered quilt. Directly beyond was the kitchen, where a single wood-fire stove stood by the rear window. Johan stepped inside. An open doorway led into Karl's bedroom; a desk rested by a window looking out over Walter's stable. Johan dropped his hat on Karl's bed and stared out at the brown hills and dotted mokala trees, the orange-blue of late morning streaked with curls of white cloud. He looked around, struck by how tidy the house was. Karl had been an organized man, but not in the usual sense; someone had cleaned the place. Johan focused his attention on the battered roll-top in the corner. Karl's desk looked heavy. Solid oak.

"Dr. Mannswell!" Adlai called from outside. "I want to show you the view!"

Johan cursed under his breath and went back through the house, joining Adlai on the shaded porch. Zithembe was dragging supplies up the dirtied slope, staging them by the porch steps.

"You can see the station-town," Adlai said, "just over there."

Johan squinted. The white outline of the town's border stood out like a chalked square amid depths of brown. Zithembe exhaled as he mounted the steps with Johan's trunk, his dark features glistening with a light sweat. The man's eyes were heavy but sharp. Calculating.

"Doctor, do you want this in the bedroom?"

Johan absorbed Zithembe's tone; did he detect a ring of indifference? The man was holding the very repository he himself had snooped through!

"You can place it beyond the door."

"I will see to Walter and get the well pumped. The oxen need to rest before we go."

"Of course," Johan said. He faced Adlai. "I'd offer you two a drink, but I'm not sure—"

"Ah, yes, I almost forgot." Adlai's spirits seemed to lift at the mention of libations. "Governor Tuner felt it uncivilized to send you out here with just the bare necessities. There's several bottles of gin, a bottle of his favorite bourbon, some wine...oh, and coffee beans, sugar, dried meats, potatoes…the Queen's been good to us."

He droned on while Johan found himself caught off-guard by the sudden vastness that settled in around him. The quiet of the wind, the great, open distances filled with nothing save those odd trees bent like crooked bones.

✦✦✦

The sun held to a rafter of hills, blushing the sky while gouging dark silhouettes into the jagged land. Johan eased back and forth in Karl's rocking chair, his heel pushing against the worn porch. He had never felt so isolated, so alone—not even on his many nights lost in the library, fettered by research. At least in those days, Sylvia would anticipate his return; now, all that awaited him was an urn. He took a pull from his pipe. The lamps needed to be lit soon, but the thought of going into Karl's home was disquieting. There was nothing of him inside, and the desk had been hell to budge. Johan set his mug of wine on the porch's drooped railing and rose to enter.

Having lit the lamps and stoked the wood stove for a little heat, Johan stood in the doorway to Karl's room, watching the deep blue of night through the bedroom window. Walter could be heard outside in his stable, lapping grimy water from the trough. Johan approached the desk and tapped his fingers on its hard oak top, frowning. He studied the wood flooring where the desk had been, keeping his eyes unfocused—a trick often used to discern unusual layers of strata. A single floorboard stood out from all the rest. Johan went to his trunk and unrolled a satchel of tools over the bed; he chose a thin spatula commonly used to pry old pottery from weak rock and returned to the board.

He slid the spatula's edge into the tight space between the boards and popped it up. A waft of chilled air rose like a sigh. Johan looked at the rectangle of darkness, then grabbed the lantern from Karl's desk. He got down on his hands and knees and reached into the floor, fishing away crumpled sheets of paper insulation as a dense object slid away from his palm. He paused, stretched his hand out, and clawed at it. Johan pushed his face to the dusty floorboards and splayed his fingers around the object, thin, covered in cloth, and hard in his grip. A shudder washed through him like the prickling sensation one feels brushing against a poisonous plant. Johan inhaled, feeling a tremble in his arm, then pulled the wrapped item out of the floor—an object as long as his forearm. He laid it next to him and studied the pain in his fingers and palm. Little droplets of blood had begun to well.

Johan hoisted himself off the floor and put the item on Karl's desk, turning to rummage through his trunk. He found his shaving bag and flicked his razor out, careful as he slit the fabric along the object's midriff, splitting the tight gauze in half.

Before him, glistening in the dull light of the lantern, lay a coal-black bone. It appeared to have small, almost indiscernible thorns rising across it like sharp hairs. Johan adjusted his glasses and bent closer. He thought it resembled a human fibula, though classifying bodily remains was an altogether different archaeological field than his. Johan stood back, engrossed with how the bone practically absorbed the light of the room, save for the hoary shine of its tiny hairs. He blinked, then gazed out of the open window. The night was quiet, the glowing stars an infinite number of deep suns. He shivered, then busied himself with a bowl for his pipe.

Johan struck a match and went to the window, puffing as moonlight beamed on the dark hills before him. If he got an early start, he could be back before anyone took notice. The coordinates in Karl's note were only a few kilometers east of here; there was no doubt they led to the dig-site. Johan peered over at the black bone on the desk, flexing his sore hand. Karl was leading him even now.

Saddling the Andalusian had been more difficult than he thought. Yet despite his bad leg causing him a rather painful mount, Johan was pleased. He inhaled the morning air and clicked his mouth, then allowed Walter to lead them down a turning descent. Johan smiled, easing on the horse's reins; it seemed the old stepper knew where they were going. Ahead, the sky turned a harsh red above the horizon. Johan tilted his hat and moved gently for his pipe; there was nothing he recalled as more satisfying than trotting with a good pipe.

Half an hour passed, and the ground flattened as the wind diminished. Far to the side of Walter's flank, the dimmest glimmer of torch-light could be seen flickering along the station-town's northern face. Walter whinnied, and Johan patted the mat of hair on his head before he checked his compass in the faint morning light. In the tall hills around him stood the black outlines of scattered mokalas, curled in the dull blue of dawn, warped watchers of his trespass. Johan put his compass away and reached for the water skin dangling from his saddle.

An hour later, Walter was taking them upward, climbing a small hill with tall pocks of dead grass that scraped at the soles of Johan's boots. As they crested the mound, the glorious arc of a deep scarlet sun peeked over the horizon, spilling a layer of crimson outward before them. Johan slid his glasses up the bridge of his nose and squinted. It was impossible to ignore the Karoo's appearance, at once both jagged and soft, dark and inviting. Perhaps it was the shade of early dawn at play with the gibbous moon, but already he could tell the land differed from that around the station-town. He wiped his forehead and motioned for Walter to rest.

At nine minutes to ten, he had already stopped to water Walter three times. The temperature had soared, and all around him, covered in the hot copper of late morning, an unusual gray grass shrugged. The dirt had taken on a purplish hue while the sky had grown odd; there was a haze to it. A firmament entirely absent of bird or insect. Johan coughed through his hand; he had become congested during the ride. Was it the climate? Perhaps the flora? He rubbed his watery eyes and heeled the stirrups, focusing on a grove of mokala trees rising like a moldy crown in the distance. Johan looked to his map and compass, juggling them as Walter clopped along.

They came off a winding slope onto the plain. Ahead, just above the trees' mangled tops, rose the tall wooded point of a winch —a cross-section of four pillars. The sight was impressive but immediately marred by a strong odor on the breeze. Even through his congested nose, the smell permeated and tickled Johan's throat. He dug into his satchel for the lavender kerchief packed from Sylvia's wardrobe and wrapped it around his face, her delicate perfume a light shield.

As he neared the grove, the sun took on a subdued, silvery hue. The wind became still, and Walter's hooves grew muted as they crunched over the gray grass, kicking up tufts of the unusual purple dirt. Johan led them into the trees and dismounted with a stiff, careful swing of his leg. He tethered Walter to one of the bent mokalas and listened to the rustle of sun-dried leaves. What was it about the air here? What was this sensation of malice coming from the trees and shade? Johan craned his neck and freed the wooden bucket tied to Walter's saddle, unscrewing another canister of water. They would be fine, so long as he kept Walter to a half canister from now on.

Johan went to the bedroll at Walter's rear and pulled out his cane, then he limped over to a shrewd mokala, where he leaned against its jagged trunk and slid down to the purple dirt. He stretched his legs out, watching in quiet as Karl's old horse lapped at the bucket of water. If not for the foul odor that hovered about the place, it would have been peaceful, even majestic, in a sense. Still, the unusual sunlight that played down through the sharp branches and ratty leaves depressed it all into an aura of uncertainty. The grove had a particular cadence to it, one not altogether natural, and the pale motes that floated in the air only bolstered that notion, like dots of snow in stasis. Johan removed his hat and allowed himself a few minutes of rest. His head was beginning to ache.

At a little past twelve, he strode into the grove and noticed hard mushrooms growing along the base of the trees. He stepped carefully, as though considerate of the soft ashen grass crackling beneath his boots. The winch could be seen a few meters off, its dark brown bulk partially obscured by a few mokalas with odd, carved markings. He steadied himself around a jutting trunk and emerged into a clearing.

Karl's site stood before him—the winch, a large A-frame tent, a charred fire pit, a planning table, and even some discarded crates broken down into a pile. But it was the earth below the winch that captured his attention, for beneath it gaped a prodigious hole close to ten meters in diameter. Most notably, there was no sign of a cave-in. Scoffing, Johan walked over to one of the winch's four pillars, each of which had been strategically anchored into the soil around the hole's circumference.

He swallowed through his swollen throat. The winch's basket had been left stationary above the ground, anchored about a meter from the hole's lip by a heavy line. Johan grabbed onto its metal side, feeling it teeter in the air, and peered over the edge into the hole as he booted a plume of purple dirt into the darkness below. Cold air rose up and brushed his clothes—the smell was unbearable! He tried to picture in his mind's eye what lay beneath him and found an image of deep, flooding ocean water. A shiver ran through him, the idea of its depth turning from a scale of meters to fathoms; he stepped back, shaking and looking about. This was not some abandoned hovel of toppled endeavor; the camp looked as though Karl had only been gone a week at most! Johan scowled and squeezed the handle of his cane, then looked over to the A-frame's green canvas. Beside it, two mokalas tugged at a mildewing hammock. How many hours had Karl swung there, contemplating his find, hiding away amid the reality of his discovery? Johan stepped back from the hole and headed for the tent but paused halfway. There was a noise in the air, a dull hum. He held his breath, listening. Distant shouting. The delayed crack of a rifle. Someone was coming.

Johan turned and shambled back to Walter. Regardless of whether or not the dig site was a focus of interest, this grove provided the only real shade for kilometers around. He labored through Sylvia's kerchief, sucking at the nauseous air. Ahead, through the parted mokalas, he saw Walter nudging at the bucket for more water. The subtle hum from beyond had risen to a light rumble, and he now heard despondent shouts.

Johan hurried through the grove and bruised his ankle on the claw of a root, panting and clutching his side as he neared Walter, his cane loose in his fingers. Walter peered up at him with water dripping from his broad lips. Johan clicked as he lugged the bucket back to the saddle. He grabbed Walter's reins and stomped clouds of purplish dirt over the wet spots of water at the base of the tree. Hooves roared through the air, seeping over and down the hills into the mokalas. Johan was in pain, his body aching, his head pounding with fever.

They made it to the clearing, where Walter paused near the excavation, shifting his long neck back and forth.

"Hallo! Komm her!"

Walter stepped forward, hesitant, his eyes rolling in his head, froth spilling from his mouth. Johan clicked and cooed, reaching his hand out, patting Walter's nose as he led him. The slow thunder of approaching hooves and garbled chatter collected at the base of the hill. Johan pulled Walter to the tent and held the canvas flap open, tapping his cane against Walter's rear and ushering him inside. At a quick glance, it appeared Karl's tent had been swept of anything pertaining to his research—no notes, no relics; absolutely nothing save a single wooden cot and a foldable writing desk. Just like the house.

Walter nudged at the tent's walls, his head only an arm's length away from the ceiling. Johan removed the kerchief from his face and wiped at his forehead. The rumbling had stopped, and in its place, a complacent chorus of bleating. A man yelled above the commotion. "In and out! Only a few minutes to prep the meat!"

A group of men shouted in response. "*Yes, sir!*"

"Then, on with it! Dismount and make haste!"

Johan's chest heaved. What was this? Walter swished his tail at the sound of whips fracturing the air, filling the grove with an agitated shuffling of corralled whines as the men outside yelled and laughed. Johan watched shadows move beyond the veil of Karl's tent. The man in charge raised his voice. "Sapper Lambert! Check the aperture's siding! Guardsman Harris! Over there!"

The hairs on Johan's neck stood on end as the breathing and murmuring of sheep became impatient amid the chatter of excited men. Johan held his breath. Footsteps in the dirt—were they coming toward him? Johan backed into Walter's flank as a large shadow fell over the tent's entry flaps. Outside, a young man grumbled to himself. "Been nothing in here for weeks...now what's the captain want with me taking a look?"

The shadow brushed aside the canvas, revealing a stout soldier in dirty khaki, his face an oval of surprise. Johan raised his hands as the man reached inside for his collar and pulled him out of the tent. He led Johan toward a group of soldiers standing around a small flock of sheep. "Oi! Captain! This old bloke was hiding in the tent with a bloody horse!"

The soldiers jeered.

"Quiet all!" A voice boomed. The grove fell silent, the only sound that of fidgeting sheep and a light wind brushing the tops of the trees. Johan swallowed, his chest heaving. The crunching grass resounded behind him like tiny glass baubles popping under a precise, deliberate weight. Johan turned around to find Captain Rael leaning against a mokala, limply pointing his Mark II Enfield at Johan's feet, a sad smirk etched on his sallow face. He lowered his pistol, shaking his head as he swiped back the tail of his red officer's coat and holstered the glistening black gun.

"Guardsman Harris," he said, "tell the men to carry on with their duties. I'll see to our German friend, from here." The captain pulled at Johan's elbow and escorted him away.

Plodding through the mokala grove, Captain Rael leaned in close to Johan's ear, his voice tired, almost soft. "You've no idea what you've done to yourself by coming here..." His words trailed off as they stepped through the trees, and the screams of whipped sheep rose toward the clouds, lost to the windy cavity of an indifferent land.

Chapter Four

GOVERNOR TUNER STRAIGHTENED A REAM OF PAPERS AT HIS WRITING desk and looked at Johan. He clasped his fingers in front of his long face and leaned in, where Johan met the gaunt man's gaze and wiped his nose. It was cold in the upstairs study, but the atmosphere was charged as if the sense of dread in Johan's chest were only a dormant sensation, estivating.

"Dr. Mannswell." Governor Tuner sighed. "Let me be clear. While you stay as our guest, I should like you to—"

"You lied to me," Johan rasped, his voice cracking with exhaustion.

Governor Tuner narrowed his eyes. "You most likely need a drink. Forgive me. It's hot out there, and I can see you've had a long day."

Johan watched as the governor moved across the study. He pulled Sylvia's lavender kerchief from around his neck and stared at a ray of sunlight beaming on the hardwood floor, its radiance plagued with hints of shadowy leaves caught in a playful breeze. He exhaled through his nose to clear its swollen passages and looked up to the painting of Teal Annayr. How it loomed above the governor's desk, the very pigments seemingly changed, rendered with the glow of some new sun having risen high above an etiolated cloud cover.

"Here. You're dehydrated." The governor held out a glass of warm water.

Johan crinkled his brow and took a long drink. "Governor, I have no motive to harm or disrupt whatever business you hold here. I only want to know where Karl is. What happened to him? What reason is there to lie to me?" Johan coughed into his hand, wheezing. "And why in God's name would you bring sheep out there?"

The governor pulled his lips from the bit of his pipe and turned to admire the large painting of Teal Annayr. The river had swollen with small rivulets of white-tipped waves. Governor Tuner whispered to himself, then turned back around to face Johan. The glint in his spider-black eyes was unsettling. "Perhaps," Governor Tuner thrummed, "I was premature in keeping a few of our...interests from you, seeing as you obviously know more than you've let on. Feel free to smoke, Dr. Mannswell."

Johan ground his teeth. "Young man, I'm not sure what you think I know, but it's evident that Karl didn't perish from a cave-in, as you would all have me believe. His excavation is intact!"

The governor regarded him with a dismissive look. "Doctor, I don't really care how you knew where to find the site. So, let's just cut to it. What do you want? Some of the artifacts?"

"What do I want? I want to know where Karl is! I want to know why you would all enact such a fallacy!"

The governor gave a weak laugh. "Let's say...security."

"Oh, security, is it?" Johan leaned forward. "What on earth could be so special out there that you would charge your liaison to preempt any questions of Karl with a lie? Where is he? What happened to him?"

Governor Tuner grinned. He rose and approached the other side of his desk and picked up Johan's glass, wiping off the wet ring it left on the finished wood with his pale, free hand. "Would you like more, Dr. Mannswell?"

Johan glared at the governor, then darted a glance at the

painting of Teal Annayr. His head and eyes became anchored as a wind caressed the tall firs at the bottom corner, where the ashen gray dyes had begun to recede in place of dark green.

Governor Tuner spoke from across the room as he poured more water. "Still fascinated with my painting, mmm?" He returned to his desk, where he towered above Johan, lank and stolid. Johan took his drink from the man's thin hand and sipped from the glass carefully. He was growing tired, his outburst having sapped what little strength he had left. Johan sat down as a cloud crossed the sun. The study grew dim, frigid, as though its veneer of welcome was suddenly washed away. It was merely a chamber now, filled with the governor's carefully placed ornaments, all set to create an elaborate scene.

"I admit," Johan said, "the piece does strike me. Yes."

Governor Tuner laughed. "Well, Dr. Mannswell, what you're looking at is a real piece of art, after all. Not that still imagery wrought by petty souls attempting to torture others with their inadequacies." The governor's demeanor changed into one of boisterous gravity, inflating the room, his arms outstretched toward Teal Annayr. "This," he said, "is how visions and dreams of that ever-common condition we know as living used to be shared…long, long ago."

Johan set his glass down with a knock. Governor Tuner whirled around. Sunlight beamed into the room once more, heating the decor and furniture back into a mask of placidity and peace, the cloud having passed.

"Governor," Johan croaked, shifting in his seat, "a painting that moves…that, shifts in color." He rubbed his eyes. "Perhaps I'm too old to be impressed with this wonder you've dredged up from God-knows-where…but I don't think the interest it demands is an entirely natural one. Please, just tell me where Karl is."

The governor's face tussled between a smile and a frown, ultimately compromising by way of a grotesque sneer; the man's incisors made him look virile, demanding. "Mr. Rynth," he said, tapping his glass with his finger, "as far as I know, is still down below, exploring his great discovery…" The governor trailed off, his gaze wandering over his desk. The study grew murky as a confluence of pipe smoke hovered in swirls and shades of blue, floating through the sunbeam at the window.

Johan's chest swelled, his head tingling. "Karl's alive…"

Governor Tuner cleared his throat. "Oh, well, he certainly might be. I don't know. I don't think either of us will know."

"What do you mean? I—"

"Dr. Mannswell, you're to go nowhere near that site. Now come, let me take you downstairs, and together we can discuss how you'll be spending the remainder of your time here. My leadership might be considered remiss by the Foreign Office were I to lose yet another German scholar…"

❦

Johan shifted on a bench in Mrs. Tuner's garden and poked his cane at the dead grass, letting the breeze brush his white hair. He had been invited to relax in the sunroom until Zithembe returned from his daily rounds, whereupon the governor would insist he be taken back to Karl's. But upon seeing the pink and turquoise decor, Johan had opted to wait outside in the fresh air. Out here, beyond the facade of the governor's hospitality and strained manners, he could enjoy a moment's respite, maybe make sense of things.

What could be so crucial that the magnates felt the need to lie to protect it? Johan coughed into his hand and wiped his forehead. What of those sheep being herded to the excavation? What purpose was there in such an act? They could graze just as well here.

Johan sighed. At least he would have a chance to be alone with Zithembe and hopefully get a few answers about the sketch in his trunk. Perhaps the man could be trusted after all; Karl may have been trying to send a message. Then there was Dr. Lasser—the only one willing to warn him.

Johan stared into the garden, his thoughts reverting to Sylvia. She would have scoffed at the flowers and flora Mrs. Tuner had planted here. Such a flagrant act of coercion to wrestle an individual's idea of beauty into the barren land. Now her garden was dried and desiccated.

Footsteps on the brown lawn roused him then. Johan turned to the manse, and his heart faltered. Edith walked toward him in a yellow sundress. Oh, she was majestic, stepping with such airs of grace and confidence—indeed the very image of Sylvia.

"Hello, Dr. Mannswell," she said, her white shoes treading weightlessly on the blanket of baked grass. Johan swallowed. She was magnificent, her bright yellow dress shining like a beacon of memories.

"Would you mind if I sat with you?" Her voice rolled over him, enchanting with a far-away warmth, as though the world itself were eager to steal the very words from her mouth.

"Not at all, mein liebling," he said, his voice faltering. Johan scooted over to make room on the bench. Edith folded the ends of her sundress against the backs of her knees and sat next to him in silence, the blue sky spread before them like an abandoned canvas. She cleared her throat as if to say something, inhaling a short breath. Johan glanced at the freckles around her nose; he would think of them later, would be compelled to.

A warm gust off the Karoo blew into the faux garden. Johan, nervous, began to make himself another pipe, then paused, turning to her. "Would this bother you?"

She smiled at him, shaking her head. He smiled back, finished pushing the tobacco into his bowl, then struck a match off the bench.

"Why do you enjoy that?" she asked.

Johan lifted an eyebrow, his lips pursed over the bit of his pipe. "I'm not really sure. I...suppose it's just a thing to do."

Edith seemed to consider his response. She rubbed her pale hands together, then looked up at him. "Do you think," she said, excited, almost out of breath, "I might have some of your pipe?"

Johan stared at her through the rim of his drooped glasses and plucked his pipe from his mouth. Edith let a quiet giggle and held it in both of her hands. She took a short drag, then let the blueish smoke float off her tongue into the breeze.

"Isn't it funny," she said, grinning, "how much I remind you of her?"

Johan's blood drained from his head.

"Karl was fond of her, too, you know. Very fond of her…" Edith began to hum, trailing off as she stared into an expired rose bush at the edge of the lawn.

Johan dipped his head some, confused and startled. Out of the corner of his eye, he studied her pale fingers clasped about the scuffed briar of his pipe. He was growing dizzy, his breathing strained. Johan glared back at her feet, watching a black ant crawl over her bare ankle, above the trim of her white shoe. The insect plodded up her porcelain skin, rounded a vein, stopped, and dug its mandibles into her.

Edith continued to hum—a broad, toothy grin on her face, her eyes little slits. "Karl…"

The sobering sense of dread Johan felt in the governor's study earlier was manifest again, only heavier. Was it mild disgust running through his stomach? Johan dragged the palm of his hand across his chin, focused on her feet. The black ant lay dead, curled into a speck.

"Do you like my feet?" Edith's voice was childish, light.

"I…believe I should go," Johan said, congested, tired. "Zithembe will be arriving soon, and…he's going to take me back to Karl's."

Edith bit her lower lip; a sliver of drool descended along the sides of her mouth. She gave a loud, pouting sigh. "Maybe I can visit?"

Johan shuddered and reached for his cane, ignoring the odd sound of her breathing—or was she panting? He avoided her gaze and squinted over the orange hills, beyond the rich umbers of Mrs. Tuner's garden, where her perennials gave way to an endless plain of dry, emaciated grass. He was trembling, his knuckles turning white from their grip on his stick.

"Johan," Edith said, drawling. "If you were to go back to that dirty hole in the ground, I could help you find him. I'm being really honest about that."

Johan turned to her, wide-eyed, strained. She suddenly seemed unreal to him—more like a shell, a hollow body with thoughts that floated as clouds do. Even her features, once so like Sylvia's, appeared off, as though sketched by a fine, albeit, rushed hand. He cleared his throat again, finding it harder to swallow. "What…"

Edith expelled a low laugh that turned into a guttural snicker. Johan became afraid of her then, of everything around him—the dead garden, the Tuners' manse, the bright and barren Karoo. He wanted to leave, to be back at Karl's, to be any place but here. He waited, uneasy in the sound of her tittering, hoping to hear Zithembe's oxen pulling up the gravel drive. Edith slid closer to him, putting her hand on his knee. He flinched.

"You *like* that part of me on your knee."

"Edith…"

"I know I could help you." Her nails clenched into his slacks, bunching the fabric. "You would *like* it if I came to visit you, Johan. Karl always did." She removed her hand and bent over, resting her head on her knees, letting her white arms dangle above the brown grass. She plied at a few of the taller strands with her long fingers. "I could catch you if you started running, you know? I could catch you." She turned her head and looked up at Johan. "Do you think Hendrik knows what Karl did to his mother?"

"Who are you?" Johan whispered. There was a burning where her nails had gouged his knee—he looked down, saw five small slits in his slacks. Edith giggled.

"You're really sick…" she said, her voice swimming off as his eyes grew heavy and a sensation of being adrift overwhelmed him.

Johan sat in a pale rowboat, the sky warped and muddled above him as he floated down a calm, emerald river. Dark forested trees hugged and shuffled from a brisk wind. He was in a valley, and the world around him was quiet, calm. Someone spoke from behind. He turned and saw Sylvia sitting aft of the stern, her skin pruned and wet. Her head of whitened hair teetered to a side as she raised a twitching arm. He thought she said something, felt a cold sigh on the nape of his neck. Johan turned and faced the bow. Edith stood bare before him, as young as Sylvia on the day they met, only odd, her features off in a way, hard to discern. She smiled at him, her dull, bottle-blond hair coiled about her face.

The rowboat tilted as Sylvia sat next to him. She put her wet hand out and took Edith's limp wrist into her bony fingers, pulling the young girl toward Johan. He stared ahead as Edith sat on the other side of him, and they rocked gently together in the quiet peace of dark trees and murky sky. Sylvia put her palm on Johan's knee as Edith's came to rest on his other. They both began to slide their fingers along his inner thigh as the river bobbed and lulled his weary head.

A fresh, uplifting wind ran at his clothes, whipping his hair and neck with playful sighs as he gave a grunt, the forests around him high and deep. He felt the boat lean as Sylvia stood, the jagged cuts at her wrists leaking a watery crimson. Johan turned his head. "Sylvia...warum hast du mich verlassen?"

She stepped away from him, lunging from the buoyant motion of the rowboat.

"Sylvia...hast du jemals einen solchen anblick gesehen?"

Johan looked at his wife, her wet skin shining like stained enamel.

"Kannst du mich anschauen, schatz?" Johan's lip quivered; she seemed unable to hear him. "Vergib mir...baby...es tut mir leid."

Sylvia's head rocked with the current, her gaze focused ahead toward the mouth of the river as overhanging trees creaked above her in a gurgling wind. A tall shape emerged in the distance—a black tower far-off in the center of a great, placid lake. Johan inhaled, the electric presence of Edith still lingering at his side. He caught the sound of sprinting in the woods then, beyond the banks of the river—something fast and massive followed their trespass into the lake. And he saw it, briefly—a colossal man as tall as the trees, lurking in the sable of the forest, wrapped in the folds of a billowing, claret cloak.

Johan gasped, turning to Sylvia. Edith was now in her place, smiling back at him in her odd grin, her neck distorted and longer than it should have been. She stepped toward him in the boat as she spoke, her voice low and layered. "You know, Karl wasn't the friend you deserved, Johan. But I could be…"

Johan stiffened as Edith put her palm on his leg, sliding her fingers into the little slits at his pants.

Chapter Five

JOHAN WAS THIRSTY, THE NIGHT AIR ON HIS SKIN HOT AND STAGNANT, the room around him quiet. He raised himself from the wet bed and reached over for his pocket watch—nothing. His leg throbbed with a sticky, prickling sensation, as though his calf-muscle rested on a branch of thorny bramble. It slowly dawned on him then that he was in Karl's bedroom, that he was breathing through his nose, that he could smell—that he actually felt good. Johan gave a low grunt and pushed against the moist sheets, sitting up. What had changed?

He licked his lips, surveying the darkened room with a squint. Where were his clothes? His glasses? Johan swung his feet off the bed, clasped his hands on Karl's writing chair, and pulled himself upright. He yawned in the moon-bright pane of a nearby window, admiring the way it cast deep blues over the hardwood floor—a lagoon by the bed.

Johan sat at the desk, his testicles hanging off the edge of the chair, that stinging sensation in his lower leg again. He grimaced while pulling up his ankle for a closer look. Waves of nausea billowed in his throat and sank to his gut—someone had tied Karl's black bone to his leg. The narrow fibula was piercing his skin, its tiny hairs needling him.

In a panic, Johan pulled at the tight gauze, his fingers pinching at the bone, feeling for any give in the cloth. He stopped as a soft pop came from the fabric; his leg momentarily burned. Johan sat back in the chair, his stomach weak and queasy, convinced the black bone had twisted deeper into his leg. It felt tighter, wound with an energy all its own. He would just have to cut the mesh then; that was the most effective way. But where were his glasses? Johan put his face close to the desktop, narrowing his gaze in the pale moonlight. No, nothing there. Perhaps the windowsill? He stood and went over, feeling a sharp bite on the bottom of his heel. Glass; the hardwood by the bed was littered with it.

Johan got down on his hands and knees and carefully felt around, the bone at his leg pulled taut and sharp. The sheer volume of glass ruled out broken spectacles, but perhaps a pitcher of water had fallen off the nightstand? Johan backed up to the foot of the bed, guessing a possible trajectory, then reached under to examine. He immediately froze. The hairs on his neck plucked up. Two glowing eyes the color of violet reflected in the lenses of his spectacles.

"Johan."

He flung himself to his feet and backed up against Karl's desk, his knees wobbling. A bored sigh came from under the bed as his glasses slid out, folded and small. Johan started to shake. "Wer ist da? Who's there?"

Silence. Then, the subtle sounds of a boat on the water, wind rippling and piping through full trees, accompanied by the notion of listing on a river beneath dark, torrid clouds, a hint of petrichor scenting the air. Johan swallowed and closed his eyes, unsure of what to do, of what hid beneath the bed. "Hello?" He whispered, rasping. "Hello?"

A low laugh emanated from the shadows, drawling and feminine. "Johan, don't you remember? We're going to help Karl…"

Johan inhaled, gripped the edge of Karl's desk. What was happening to him? Was he with fever? He felt wholly elsewhere, in a place vaguely familiar yet drowned in the heavy nostalgia of a dream that washed over him.

"Pick them up," the voice said. "Pick them up and put them on…"

Panting, Johan bent down and picked up his glasses.

"You should probably get dressed and go to Karl, don't you think? He's waiting…"

Johan wiped the sweat from his brow, dazed. He stumbled his way into the main room, past the squat sofa, and into the small cooking area in the back, where he lit the lamp on the table and took Karl's ladle off a hook on the wall. He dipped the wooden spoon into a basin of water and drank, allowing the liquid to run down his chin and chest. The front door opened behind him. Johan's arm shook, the ladle quivering at his lips.

"I'll see you there," the voice whispered. The front door closed with a creak—footsteps receded off the porch. Johan dropped the wooden spoon and limped toward the front door, swinging it open to the subdued, maudlin sounds of the Karoo in a deep sleep.

☙❧

Johan discovered his dirty clothes folded on a stool at the foot of Karl's bed and his cane on the floor. Someone brought him back here, undressed him, left water on the nightstand, and tied the black bone to him. He sat at the foot of the bed and pulled his leg up, having cut away the gauze with his shaving razor. He pinched at the bone as it twisted into his skin, and the dull sheen of its hairy barbs flickered in the lamplight.

"Scheisse!"

Johan threw his hands down and stomped his foot on the floor. The bone was digging into him; he bit his thumbnail. The station-town was a long walk; without a horse, it might take him close to three hours. He stared at his leg. The sight of the black bone fastened around his calf, slightly depressed into it—he had to get to Dr. Lasser's. Perhaps the young man could help him, maybe even answer a few questions.

Johan bent over and grabbed his clothes off the stool. He put his pants on and wangled a dirty sock over the protrusive black bone at his ankle. Once dressed, he patted his vest for his pocket watch and Karl's letter. The letter was safe, but his watch had stopped—and where was his pipe? Disoriented, he made for the kitchen to pack a few provisions. If he left in the next hour, he might beat the rising sun.

❦

Karl's home stood in bleak contrast to the white moon—a silhouette, dimmed and quiet. The black bone was uncomfortable, but he tried his best to ignore it and focus on the feel of his cane in his hand, how it conjured old comforts and aroused the idea of a silent partner with which he kept company. Johan inhaled the stale, warm air and turned his back on Karl's house. He thought of Edith, of how that strange girl made him tingle—and that dream, those eyes under the bed.

Johan adjusted his glasses. The station-town sat below in a crook of hills. He listened to the crackle of dried grass beneath his boots, relishing the plod of his cane in the dirt as he looked out to the rows of housing beyond the station town's walls. There Dr. Lasser kept his residence—somewhere.

An hour later, the moon remained bright, spreading its frosted hue over the ridges and bumps that rose in magnified shades of black and gray. He felt he traversed the moon itself—would it not look like this? Feel like this? Johan stepped into a clearing, swept the ground with the heel of his shoe, and sat down in the dirt. He took a large swig from the water flask and wiped his forehead. Sensing the bone as it nibbled into his weakened calf muscle—the slightest touch of a needle in the hollow of a tooth—he leaned back some and stretched his leg.

He began to wonder about finding Dr. Lasser's house. But if Adlai could be believed, no one else had taken up residence in the adjacent units outside of town. So perhaps the young doctor would be up late with a lamp, his nose in his books. Johan smirked to himself, remembering all those years ago when he and Karl attended university, when they had been so young as to make a lazy

68

game of seeing who could stay awake the longest, who would get the furthest in their studies. Of course, once they met Sylvia, they started playing a different game.

Johan wiped his nose in the dark, surrounded by a chorus of long-horned grasshoppers. The pinpoint glow of the town's torches gave rise to his desire for a pipe. Irritated, he took a pull from the flagon of water instead, his memories coming on a bit stronger than he liked.

In the end, Sylvia did not love Karl. And one cannot choose who they fall in love with any more than the sun can help but rise —oh, but Karl had been so disparaged over this! And it was no coincidence when he too volunteered for the recently established Deutsche Morgenländische Gesellschaft. Of course not. Karl was pointed enough to know that if he wanted to remain in Sylvia's proximity, he would need to shadow Johan's academic pursuits. And they had been happy for a while, the three of them. But, when they were selected to lead their first dig—India no less!—it came to be that Sylvia was with child. Karl never outwardly blamed Johan for staying in Berlin, but Johan felt it; that final wedge between them. He did what he could for Karl, even going so far as to push the society's popular monograph series, Abhandlungen für die Kunde des Morgenlandes, to publish news of his dig.

Johan frowned in the night, recalling how that had only worked to lead Karl further away. For, in Karl's view, he had been made to be alone; abandoned, as it were, on a far shore, tricked by fate, while the woman he loved shared a child with another man—his friend, his colleague.

Johan ran his tongue over his teeth, his understanding of old events as potent as aged wine. But did Karl not find his own stride in the end? Even succeeding so far as to excavate a heretofore unknown site near that ancient city of Thatta several years later? Obviously, the man should have been replete with satisfaction, with victory, and yet, for reasons unknown, Karl loosened specific protocols and pushed for more extraneous excavation. Ultimately his choices culminated in the deaths of three field students. His expulsion from the society was prompt, and all mention of his deeds were effaced.

Johan took another sip of water, raised his eyes to the stars, and sighed. The sweat on his brow had dried; the scent of kikuyu grass carried on an oncoming breeze. The land was quiet as he rose, the outline of the station-town marred by a dingy mokala some meters away. The draft scuppered to a calm then, and Johan pushed on the ridge of his spectacles until the lenses touched his lashes. He peered into the shadowy grades, studying everything from the bent tree to the lanky grass to the murky ridges. Johan gripped his cane, exhaling amid the sound of sawing grasshoppers and swaying branches—a whisper in the calm night:

"*Johan.*"

He froze, listening as the dried grass compressed under a weight in the darkness—a patter of feet in the dirt, then a shaking of the mokala's tattered leaves. Johan poised himself, slouched with his cane in both hands, facing the tree. He watched as the leaves parted, and a pair of sparkling, violet eyes stared out at him.

"*Karl fickte deine frau…*"

A lie.

"*Sie liebte ihn in ihrem arsch, Johan…*"

A lie!

"*Sylvia liebte es…*"

"Nein!" Johan yelled. "Stop it!" He raised his cane and slashed at the air, then slouched, panting, out of breath, his chest heaving as a rustle in the grass came from below the tree. He grimaced in the sound's direction, seeing violet eyes shining through strands of a desiccated brush. Johan put his hand to his head, dropping his cane. The violet eyes lifted, rising from the grass. They stared out at him from the dark fabric of a body: a young woman. Edith came toward him under the broken shadow of the mokala, her face aglow in silver moonlight as she touched the bark of the twisted tree with her hand.

"Johan," she said, "I thought you were going to the grove, to the hole. This isn't the way there."

"Edith..." Johan inhaled, confused, his eyes wide. "I...were you...was that you under the bed?"

Edith shrugged her shoulders, put her hands behind her back, and skipped in his direction, kicking dirt behind her heels. Her countenance disturbed him—shaky and skewered as if the lines of her face were unsure where to begin and end. Johan stepped back, the bone at his leg burning hot, grinding.

"Go to the hole," she said, coming closer, gazing up at him.

"What is this? What are you?"

Edith gave a laugh. "Sal wanted me to end you, Johan. Governor has no patience for a bumbling old man, it seems."

"I don't understand what's happening..."

"Oh, of course not. Karl did, though. He knew quite well." Edith flashed a broad smile and darted just below Johan's chin. She stretched onto her toes and pecked him on the neck with cold lips. "I've disobeyed him. The governor."

Johan winced as her fingers dug into his arms. The young woman held him close to her; the scent of dry mulch wafted from her nostrils and mouth. "Why do you look like her?" he asked. "Why do you look so much like my Sylvia?"

"Your Sylvia?" Edith released him and stepped back, the edges of her face calmer, settled. "Don't you mean Karl's Sylvia?"

Johan sank to the dirt, indifferent to the pain this caused his leg.

"Ah, so you thought you knew." Edith knelt down beside him and ran her hand through his gray hair. "He betrayed me too, you know. His interests harm those who are overly trusting, Johan. The pure." Edith sucked through her teeth. "I once asked for his help in finding something of mine...and in return, I was to help him understand..."

"Understand what?" Johan whispered.

"The reality of the past. A reality none have been able to realize." Edith ran her fingers down Johan's cheek and lifted his face to hers. "Help me. Help me, and I can help you..." She kissed him on the lips.

Johan whimpered, exhausted. "What am I supposed to do?"

"You need to go to the hole. You need to get below and find Karl. The old man has what is mine—what he promised me."

Johan licked his lips, his eyes strained and out of focus on Edith's moving face. "What...what did he promise you? What does he have?"

Edith's mouth quivered, all at once stretching and gaping. "Bones." Her violet eyes flashed to his bent leg in the dirt. "Like that one."

Johan moved his leg, pulled it underneath him.

Edith stood erect in the moonlight. "Go to the hole, Johan. There's nothing up here for you."

"How...how do I get this off? I don't want it on me. I'm tired..."

"You're not getting it off. Go to the hole."

"Sylvia—" Johan shook his head. "Edith, help me..."

"But if I'm gone too long, the governor will hurt me." Edith's chin convulsed. "He's good at hurting. Please, go to the hole and make your way down. We can help each other there. It's safe and warm, and no one will bother us."

"I have to get this off!"

Edith swung her arm around the back of Johan's neck, clamping his head into her taut bosom. "You're not getting it off. Do you understand? It's been allowed to make a home in you."

Johan gurgled, unable to breathe, his hands clawing at her waxy arm. His leg scuffled out from beneath him as he struggled to rise. Edith pushed down on him, a grunt burping from her throat. "You're not even half the man Karl was," she said. "No wonder Sylvia—"

Johan flexed, then stomped on the dirt. His leg inflated as the bone twirled against his calf muscle, and he rose with a yowl. Edith stumbled backward into the clearing, her face amused. She laughed. "Oh, go on then! Talk with the Sri Lankan! But he's a liar, Johan! He's a little liar, and he'll tell you I'm no good..." Edith bared her teeth at him and swished her dress with her hips. "Go on, go play with him!" Her lips then formed into an exaggerated pout. "Just hurry...I need you."

Johan caught his breath as Edith walked off into the Karoo toward the station-town. He looked down at his leg, astonished and afraid.

The row of vacant homes outside the station-town sat beneath looming dawn, their roofs angled with dark-blue shadows. Johan glanced at the stalks of grass behind him—still no sign of her violet eyes. With a sigh, he squatted, ran a hand through his hair, and reached for the flask of water at his side. Taking a sip, he gazed off to the white walls of the station-town—into the dim, empty confines of its derelict buildings.

Johan holstered the flask and made a dash for the adjacent row of houses. Safe on the far side of the first home, he took a breather, leaning against the sanded wood paneling. Ahead, the Karoo stretched dull and foreboding in the early morning. He felt like a man on the edge of the world, the empty home at his back the last hiccup in a long series of attempts to structure nature's sprawl. Johan wiped his face and went to the rear of the house, where a shallow set of steps led to a narrow wooden door beside a large window. He peered through the uneven panes. The place was dark and barren, not a single bit of furnishing inside.

He stepped back, checking the next home and the next, until he was at the last in the row, the dawn and moon both reflected in a sort of moment-less schism on its slanted, murky windows. Johan made his way to the porch, his palm on the flask at his waist to steady it from clanking—were those wind-chimes he heard? Johan stopped, keeping himself as dwarfed as possible. Yes. Above the crackle of the station-town's torches, the soft chime of scaled notes came from the house's deck.

Johan made his way around, his chest welling with hope. Rounding the corner, he saw a dim orange glow at the kitchen window. He smiled; it was just like he imagined—the young man was awake through the hours of darkness, buried in study. Johan crept closer to the back steps. He lifted his foot and paused as the wood beneath his shoe creaked. Johan took another step and raised his eyes to the windowsill.

Dr. Lasser sat in his kitchen at a littered table under the dim light of an unseen lamp. Around the man lay a messy clutter. Strewn books and piled clothes; shelves along the walls, all stuffed with books and esoteric objects; daggers and maps; scrolls of parchment; collectibles; masks. The place was a menagerie of the arcane.

Johan took a deep breath and tapped at the window with his cane. Dr. Lasser jumped to his feet, the pen in his hand falling from parted fingers. The young doctor stood wide-eyed, pale and sallow despite his tanned skin. Johan tapped again, and Dr. Lasser moved toward the window, poised, peering with caution into the glass, his shaky hands reaching for the latch. As he swung the window ajar, Johan thrust the handle of his cane onto the sill.

"Dr. Lasser," he croaked, "I trust this isn't a bad time?"

☙❧

The house was warm, the smell inside fusty from a stagnancy of rotted food and diluted soap-water. Johan sat at the kitchen table, rubbing his leg.

"Is there anything else?" Dr. Lasser leaned against the counter, arms crossed, his thin figure blocking the glow of a lantern.

"No," Johan said. "Everything I've told you is as I recall it."

Dr. Lasser nodded and unfolded the sleeves of his wrinkled shirt, then turned to the cabinets, a sense of purpose having settled into his demeanor. "Well, first thing's first," he said, "I've some old ruby around here. It's been opened…but should do just fine. Stuff rarely turns out here. And second, you need to avoid Edith at any cost."

Johan let a smile crack his face and gazed into the gloomy main room, trying to discern the various objects littered on the bookshelves; such relics seemed better suited for a home like his own—or Karl's. Johan set his teeth as his mind's eye lent an image. He adjusted his glasses and looked at the doctor, busying himself with the port. Then he lowered his stare to the clutter on the table. It lay messed with illegible papers, some torn through by the tip of a dried pen, their leaves partially covering a moldy loaf of bread. He reached out with his hand and plied away a soft-backed book to reveal an old periodical stained with rings of coffee or tea. Johan picked it up and turned it over—an issue of Abhandlungen für die Kunde des Morgenlandes.

Dr. Lasser set down two smudged glasses of a thick, black drink. He then handed one to Johan and took a seat across from him. His eyes moved to the booklet in Johan's fingers. Dr. Lasser took a sip from his glass. "Unfortunately, my German is lacking enough to where I couldn't read that one," he said.

Johan laid the periodical down and stared at him. "Why is your house filled with Karl's things?"

Dr. Lasser blinked. "To understand what Karl found—what he unleashed. Zithembe helped me gather it all. He's to be trusted, Dr. Mannswell. As is the captain."

"But Zithembe serves Mr. Courner...and Captain Rael."

"Oh no, Zithembe serves himself." Dr. Lasser's eyes widened. "Don't mistake his presence here as anything other than a means to an end. Now, I couldn't really say just what that end is, but it goes against Sal's. Believe me, the governor has only made matters worse. Otto knows that. He's playing his part well."

"What do you mean?"

"Dr. Mannswell, I worked with Karl. But Zithembe, his people apparently knew something of what Karl found. The two of them were already quite close before I came into the picture. And what Karl did by uncovering what lay below...well, in the end, their efforts to mitigate—to correct—that error...ultimately failed. Governor Tuner took over the excavation. With Edith's help, of course. Why should you suspect Zithembe? The captain I can see, but Zithembe?"

Johan raised an eyebrow. "I'll keep my suspicions to myself if it's all the same."

"Alright," Dr. Lasser said. "Very well. I understand you've come into all this quite blind."

Johan folded his arms and ran his tongue over his teeth. The men sat in quiet as a pair of small birds chirped outside in the early dawn.

"Can I see it?" Dr. Lasser motioned to Johan's leg. "Karl showed it to me once, but…I wasn't allowed to touch it."

Johan studied the thin man, how the shadows on his face lurched and waned from the flickering lamplight. In the kitchen window, hues of brown could be noticed behind him, heating up in color from the brightening sky. Dr. Lasser leaned back in his chair. A subtle twitch had developed below his jawline, jumping and jerking in his neck—a stressed vein, most likely.

"You'll remove it, yes?" Johan held the doctor's gaze.

"I'll do what I can, Dr. Mannswell, but I'll need to see it first."

"Of course." Johan pinched his nose. "Right." He stuck his leg out and inched up his pants. Dr. Lasser lowered his head over the table and narrowed his eyes despite the daylight easing into the kitchen. "Interesting," he said. "There's no blood, no swelling…just a shallow depression in the skin." He sat back and looked at Johan. "I believe I see why Karl didn't want me touching it."

"And why is that?" Johan murmured, lowering his pant leg.

Dr. Lasser sipped his port and scratched his cheek. "Well, Karl kept it wrapped in several layers of gauze and cloth, but he always had it on his person, either at his belt or in his pack. Yet he never allowed it to come into contact with his skin…I expect for this very reason."

Johan flared his nostrils. "Why then, for the love of God, would Zithembe tie it to my leg?"

Dr. Lasser's brow turned solemn and somber. "You really think he did this to you? What reason could he possibly have?"

Johan's head was beginning to hurt. "What possible reason could anyone have? Please! I just want it off!"

Dr. Lasser leaned back with a sigh. "You're not in any immediate pain, are you?"

"It's minimal."

"Well, that's good…Dr. Mannswell, I can try to remove it, but I'll be honest…I'll need to make lacerations. I'll also need to administer a generous dose of morphia to subdue the pain. Are you okay with that?"

"Just get the damned thing off me…"

"Very well, but I'll need more light to perform the procedure. So, while we wait for the sun to rise, I'll brew us some tea, and…I suggest you listen while I fill you in on certain events. You need to know what's been happening here."

"By all means." Johan clipped the words, terse. The pain in his head was now a steady throb, pounding at his temples.

Dr. Lasser gave an assenting nod and rose to dig through his cabinets. He spoke over his shoulder. "I suppose I should start with how I came to be here…"

"I arrived in late November of last year under orders from the Foreign Office. It was all rather bizarre, now that I think back on it. But war is an odd endeavor in and of itself, and seeing as this most recent one was nearing its end, I left my post in the Transvaal rather elated and came to the coordinates they'd listed in their letter. I was, of course, told to tell no one but instead pass along the proper discharge papers I'd been sent. Karl's excavation was well underway by the time I came, and after about a week of my settling in and getting acquainted with the station-town—"

"Do you not know the name?" Johan interrupted.

Dr. Lasser gave a nervous smile. "Of the town? No…no, I'm not sure anyone does…maybe Karl, maybe Sal…"

Johan rubbed his chin as Dr. Lasser continued. His head felt as if it would crack.

"…in any event, one day I was called out to Karl's site. There'd been an accident, you see. Now, I'd heard word of something going on outside of the town, somewhere in the Karoo. What I saw, though, as I'm sure you know, was very surprising indeed. Back then, the illness hadn't spread yet and—"

"You mean the Influenza outbreak."

Dr. Lasser sighed and scratched his head. "No…Dr. Mannswell,

I'm sorry, there's a lot I'm still trying to make sense of myself, but… no, we're not dealing with the common cold here. You must understand, everyone is sick. Governor Tuner, Captain Rael, Adlai, myself, the citizens…*you*."

"What do you mean? Sick with what?" Johan was growing irritable.

"It came from below. From that hole in the ground. So Karl, by all rights, would've been the first to contract it. Yes? You'd think. But…no, he had an immunity…" Dr. Lasser looked closely at Johan's leg. "An artifact he kept tightly bound in cloth…"

"I don't think I follow…"

"You will," Dr. Lasser said, gesturing with his hand. "Don't worry." He finished the remainder of his port and wiped his mouth with his wrinkled sleeve. "The winch had just been completed, I learned, and on that day, while lifting and anchoring its four supports into the soil around the excavation, one of Karl's men had taken a misstep and gotten wound in a bit of line. His leg was broken above the knee. I administered a degree of morphia, set his leg right, and told Karl the man would have to recover back in town, that I could take him back with me. Karl thanked me and, with the journey to town being as long as it is, offered to share what he was working on while my horse rested. He led me into his tent, whereupon I was introduced to Edith…"

Johan perked at this. "What was she doing?"

"She was sitting at his desk, reading a piece of paper with some odd language on it. I don't really recall. But I do remember she began to protest when Karl insisted she leave. With her gone, he proceeded to show me several daguerreotypes he'd taken from below…Dr. Mannswell, the amount of light he had to employ to register an image down there at all was impressive enough, but what he *captured*…" Dr. Lasser let out a long breath. "My God…slabs of dark stone, open spaces…"

Johan put his elbows on the table and clasped his hands beneath his chin. "What did Karl find?"

"I don't know," Dr. Lasser said, "it's extraordinary though…a structure of some kind…but more importantly, I believe it's where that bone in your leg came from. Don't you get it? That bone is how Karl was able to ward off the illness!"

The lines in Johan's face crinkled. "This illness you keep mentioning—"

"Yes, yes." Dr. Lasser sniffed. "I'll get to that. Trust me, you should be fine for the time being. Now, later that night, after I'd returned to town and settled the injured man inside my makeshift clinic, I developed a cough. The next day, I was with fever. The injured man? He overheated in the night, and in the morning, I had him declared dead. The following day, what would be the third day, after administering several medicines to myself, and with no relative improvement, what should happen? Karl sends for me, something of dire importance, I was told. So, sickly, sedated, and begrudgingly, I took my carriage to his dig site…and do you know what happened when I neared that hole in the ground? When I entered that strange mokala grove? I felt alive. I felt better and clearer the closer I got to that giant orifice."

Johan spoke carefully. "Doctor, what I think you're proclaiming is that this illness somehow acts like an addiction?"

"Yes! But it's a disease, Dr. Mannswell! And once exposed to it, you must ingest it regularly or die from withdrawal." Dr. Lasser squeezed his eyes shut. "Consequentially, it seems only those of us that directly visited the site came down with its purest form—oh, it was spread to the other residents in town just out of sheer proximity, albeit in a somewhat mutated fashion. And I know my bringing it back with me that particular day helped in this regard…but my biggest fear? My biggest fear is that it may give rise to an awful pandemic sometime in the next decade or two. Who knows where all the remaining residents went off to on that last train out of here…they all had such a weak semblance of the illness, so it *was* rather flu-like in its symptoms…but it will never go away for them… it will change and morph and spread like any good virus does."

"Dr. Lasser," Johan said, a tone of incredulity to his voice.

"Strange?" Dr. Lasser gave a crooked grin. "Yes. You want to call it all strange, don't you? Well, you're right. It is very strange. Listen. Do you know why Karl called me back to his site that day?

He confessed this to me! It's because he was testing a supposition of his. For quite some time, he suspected the illness worked in the manner it does. Only he wasn't sure! After all, he had that bloody bone to protect him! But Karl, always practical, always thoughtful, considered his workers might get sick, and so he forbade them from coming into town until he was sure…"

"Why did he wait? What changed? Surely other men had been injured before you arrived."

"Apparently…he was waiting for me—a doctor. I was hand-picked, Dr. Mannswell. I was…*selected*."

"Selected…Dr. Lasser, this is quite—"

"Karl worked for someone…an organization as old as the church. He never told me any more than that, but I was seemingly chosen when the time was right. Now, after this was all revealed to me, after a brief spell of anger on my part, we began to meet daily to work out a method of bypassing the illness's negative effects—naturally ferrying the infected back to his dig site on a daily basis was out of the question."

Johan put his hand to his forehead and rubbed his eyes.

"…at first we filled wagons with soil from around the hole and made gardens with it back in town. We had hoped that in time we could grow vegetables, *serve the cure*, so to speak, in stock and broths and whatnot. Didn't take, I'm afraid. The illness comes from the air —that cold draft seeping up from below. So, we…took to infecting our livestock. Zoonosis, Dr. Mannswell! The virus infects both animals and men! So, we would infect the sheep and harvest the meat, serving it in town. And it worked! For a while, we had men coming to and fro between the site and station-town without any mishaps…we had a temporary system that worked. But after Karl went down that last time…it all changed. He never came back. Without him, Sal took control of the dig and tripled the cost of the meat." Dr. Lasser lowered his head. "A third of our population died, Dr. Mannswell. Those too poor, those that stole…those that killed. And dammit if that little wench didn't plant those ideas in Sal's head!"

Johan sat up. "You mean Edith. Why do you say that? Why do you call her a wench? She's just a girl."

"Dr. Mannswell, she's not natural! There's something off about her! Tell me you see it. Think! Where did Karl find her? What could she possibly know of what Karl was working on? Why does she resemble your wife so? *Why* was she out there in the Karoo with you last night? Those dreams of yours…I've read of a similar account in one of Karl's books. An old tome he acquired in the Carpathians some years ago. I'll show it to you afterward—it's in my bedroom. But Dr. Mannswell, it details similar visions…do you understand? You're not the first to have experiences like the ones you're having! It could provide answers!"

"Doctor," Johan grumbled, "I'm not sure what an old book could tell me about these dreams of mine, and I know you pulled me aside after the governor's dinner…but if you're so against the man's practices, why stay? Why not leave this place and acquire help elsewhere?"

"Because we're dealing with dangerous entities here. A certain enterprise with more bearing than just this little mock town. It spans continents, kingdoms, and governments. I told you, Karl was employed by it…a society, an ancient lacework of robust design…"

Johan stared at the young doctor across from him, listening to the hiss of the dull lamp on the counter, its flame a low flare in the sheen of morning light. Dr. Lasser fidgeted with his hands beneath the table as his eyes darted about.

"Well." Johan cleared his throat. "Be that as it may, do you maybe think it's bright enough for you to get this bone off me? I believe it's hurting my head…I'm…nauseous…" Johan let out a breath and slumped back in his chair. His vision was blurred, the images before him broken into wet shards.

"I'll remove it for you," Dr. Lasser whispered. "I will. But afterward, I need to find an answer to what Karl loosed on us…Dr. Mannswell, if that excavation is closed off, if the hole in the ground were to cave-in, the source of the illness would be trapped, and all of us would die in the next few days without it. I can't allow that…

but if I had the bone or just a piece of it…it might lead to a cure…
if just a biotic tincture at first…but it would give us time."

"What did you put in my drink?" Johan winced as he tried to sit
up. Breathing was difficult.

"Laudanum. I'm sorry I didn't tell you, but you'll most likely be
out soon, and I'll get to work. Please, don't mistake my intentions. I
want to solve this together, but…trust works both ways, Dr.
Mannswell. I can already see what she's doing to you. Understand,
I'd thought you dead. I'd received word you were caught at the dig
site by Otto, that he brought you to Sal afterward…the captain
expressed his regret, but we're playing high stakes here. He's been
ordered to watch the dig site full-time now, poor fellow…faith in a
stranger is just so hard to come by out here." The doctor cocked an
eye at Johan. "I knew for certain Sal would have that girl kill you.
Appears she took an interest in you, though…" Dr. Lasser got up
from his chair and came around the table. He pulled Johan to his
feet and led him through the kitchen into a side room, removing his
dusty coat. "This is where I'll take it out. When you wake, we can
discuss our next steps." The doctor brought Johan to a tall cot
beneath a large window filled with sunlight. He laid him on his back
and pulled off his shoes. "I've no idea how long this will take, and
I'll be careful not to rush it, but if I catch you stirring, I'll have to
put you back to sleep with a dose of ether…"

Johan felt his head sink into a pillow as Dr. Lasser took his
glasses and put them on the windowsill. The doctor's almond
features wavered above him, narrowed and shifting, out of focus,
retreating farther away as the flicker of a scalpel beamed across his
face.

Johan roused on the cot, his leg a dull throb. He smacked his lips
and turned his head, resting his cheek against the pillow to face the
window above him. A harsh sunset had come over the Karoo,
casting the bedroom in a brilliant red. His throat was parched. "Dr.
Lasser," he said, his eyes heavy. "Doctor, how long have I been

asleep?" The room was quiet, save for the low hum of insects outside the window. Johan sat up with a subtle awareness of being alone. As his senses labored to survey the room—to register what lay before him, slumped against the wall—he gradually took-in that a metallic tray and several surgical blades were scattered along the floor. Johan pinched his eyes, unsure of what he saw on the other side of the room as he reached for the windowsill and felt for his glasses. Slowly, he put them on and chanced a proper look. Dr. Lasser was sprawled by the door, motionless, his head lolled back as the black bone protruded from his mouth.

Johan felt his body vibrate. His breaths became short and shallow. He put his hand to his chest—was this panic? Johan fought to gain control of himself, and after his chest stopped heaving, he removed the sheet covering his legs. His joints were stiff, but there were no cuts where the bone had been, just a shallow trench-like groove in the side of his calf muscle. Johan lowered his feet to the floor and wobbled over to Dr. Lasser. The man's mouth had been torn and battered from the barbs of the bone; small flecks of enamel littered his swollen lips. Johan lowered his eyes to the doctor's hand, where an object rested clenched in his fist. Reluctantly, Johan pried the young doctor's fingers loose. A shiver ran the length of his spine—his pipe lay in the man's palm, its bowl still full of semi-burnt tobacco. Johan wiped his face with the back of his wrist. Hesitant, he picked up his pipe and stuffed it in his vest.

Feeling sick, he retreated back to the cot and moved it aside, opening the bedroom window. Air off the Karoo eased inside, fluttering over the doctor's loose papers. Johan inhaled, somewhat strengthened by the familiar smells of burnt grass and warm dust, then spotted his coat on a set of drawers in the corner of the room and hobbled over to dig for his pouch of tobacco. Soon, he was seated on the cot, puffing with an appetite.

Why put laudanum in the port? Had he and Dr. Lasser not come to an agreement? Why the trickery? Johan's gaze was drawn to the black bone. It seemed Edith had been right—the doctor was a liar. Perhaps she really was the one who wished to help him. But trust worked both ways, did it not? And Karl had left the bone in his care for a reason. Maybe it was time to accept her, to actively listen to what she was trying to tell him. Johan took a pull from his pipe and exhaled a cloud of smoke into the red room, his thoughts meandering now—just how often *had* Karl and Sylvia been left alone? Was it really possible? He shook his head and tapped out the ash from his pipe. Either way, getting back to the dig site was paramount. Karl could be alive.

Johan stood and approached the doctor. The stench off of his body was pungent—the release of his bowels a dull, persistent mark in the room. Johan held his breath as he knelt down and stuck his fingers into the doctor's mangled mouth. He had to be delicate with where he put pressure on the black bone—its little hairs were sharp. Johan pulled back on it, skinning his fingers against the doctor's broken teeth. Flexing his hand, he tried again, ignoring the pressure of Dr. Lasser's throat—oh, but it was palpable, running up his wrists and into his shoulders, sinking through his heart and into his stomach!

Taking a deep breath, Johan carefully gave a yank. A waft of air rose out of the doctor's throat. Johan stumbled backward and stuck his face through the open window, inhaling reprieve from the sour smell inside. He looked down at the black bone in his hand, surprised to find a sensation close to pleasure subtly register along the length of his arm.

A curious smirk formed at his lips as he sat down on the cot. Johan shivered, feeling a well of gravity below his feet. Moving his fingers around the bone sent ribbons of excitement through his body, his head. Oh, a stream of air in his lungs—like the small clouds of a miniature heaven, a microbial Holy chorus humming within him!

Chapter Six

Dr. Lasser's body had come to resemble something of a prehistoric fish to Johan—a mythical monster dredged up from deep within the sea. Already flies were darting about the blood and broken teeth of his mouth, matting themselves among the strands of his thick, black hair. Johan ignored the buzzing as he stared out of the window, his eyes heavy and sincere, focused on the dark spread of a blithe Karoo.

A plume of dirt had risen in the distance, a vaporous puff arching above the crimson line of dying sunlight, trailing into the deep blue of night—a rider, possibly a courier of some sort. Johan followed their trajectory as he listened to the croon of late evening, inhaling the scent of dried grass as it lingered about the room. With a turn from the window, he left, shutting the door behind him before he dug in his vest for matches. He ignited the lantern at the kitchen counter and adjusted its flame to a low flare, then walked through the main room, noting Karl's antiques on the shelves as his socked heels wracked the wooden floor. After giving a few of the items a passing appraisal, he continued on to Dr. Lasser's bedroom. Hopefully, the book the young man mentioned would be easy to find.

Standing in the doorway, he held the lamp out, letting its glow reconcile with the darkness inside. A set of cream-colored curtains had been drawn against the room's only window, and where the doctor's twin bed occupied the far corner, a medley of books had been stacked as tall as the mattress. Johan set the lantern down on Dr. Lasser's writing desk—a small battered thing nestled beside the doorway.

Johan approached the bed and crouched down with a sigh. He began to pick through the anemic volumes. From what he could tell, each was an out of date study concerned with geography around a particular choice of river systems: French, German, Italian, Spanish, Greek, Latin—an incredibly old one on the Nile, another on the Danube, several to do with the Carpathian Mountain range. But where was the tome Dr. Lasser mentioned? Johan sat back on his haunches. Abruptly, he stood and went back to the lamp on the desk, and by way of its light, spotted a shallow under-drawer. He pulled at the ivory knob—locked—then, clenching his hand, he plied his fingertips under the drawer's lip and yanked, snapping it off its tracks to the floor. Johan bent down and smirked to himself. Coddled in the drawer lay a thick, leather-bound book in large octavo. With a delicate hand, he plucked up the tome and opened its fragile cover:

Nou Explorare de Vechi Lume
de
Magnus Dux Gri Irion de Alabastru Grup
MDCLXXXVII
provence de Cluj-Napoca

Johan flipped through a few of the pages—the room quiet as if to make way for the cackle of moving paper. He realized the book pertained to Africa—to this very region. Johan lowered the text under the lamp to find a sheet of notepaper had been placed in between the pages near the back. He gently parted the book. The handwriting was Karl's. Johan brought the paper closer to his face:

. . .

...by Irion's account, Ghadra Nine would appear to be near modern-day Kimberly. He has supposed it may contain linkage with Ghadra One, which lies farther south still. However, not all keys grant entry. But, as Ghadra Three's brought me this far, I trust Ghadra Nine will contain the very same in comparison. I wonder, will it be an arm I find? Perhaps I'll get lucky and discover that all I'll need is a rib...

Johan heard a click on the porch outside. He held his breath and listened. An uneasy sensation crept over him as if he were in the company of someone unseen. The doctor's wind-chimes had picked up in their rhythm, so perhaps it was the breeze. Johan sighed and turned toward the middle of the tome, catching several plated illustrations interspersed throughout the text. He backtracked to the closest one. Johan's brow furrowed in confusion. The plate seemed to have to do with astronomy, yet the stars it depicted were clearly wrong. Johan rubbed his eyes. Celestial bodies had never been his forte and only interested him during university for their crucial connection to his terrestrial studies. After all, ancient civilizations had thrived from their understanding of space, so if he was to be apt at his job, it was crucial he familiarize himself with the firmament. Perhaps these were misunderstood constellations of the Southern Hemisphere?

A loud succession of knocks at the front door reverberated through the home, and Johan quickly turned the knob at the lantern and extinguished its flame. He heard the shuffling of boots on the porch while he stood in the darkness, his heart throbbing. Another knock then—followed by a voice.

"Samith?"

Johan's chest constricted; it was Adlai.

"We need to discuss the German...Otto's man said he's gone. Old boy's not at Karl's anymore—c'mon now, open up!"

Johan listened to the footwork outside. It was hard to tell for sure, but Adlai seemed to be alone.

"Goddammit, man! Open up!"

Adlai pounded on the door again. There was some muffled talking, followed by a suppressed cough as Johan wiped at his face in the trapped heat of the house. So there were others out there beside Adlai. Johan rubbed his beard, nervous. How long could he realistically avoid the station-town's grip? What was stopping these men from coming inside? Johan prepared himself for the inevitable clack of the door's knob being turned but instead heard the retreat of boots as the porch fell silent. He exhaled, the buzz of spent adrenaline spreading from his head, tingling his temples.

"Sylvia," he whispered, putting his face in his hand, "ich bin mude…was mache ich?"

The room grew hotter around him. No doubt someone would be back to check in on Dr. Lasser. Johan stepped into the main room and peered out at the kitchen window. A faint glimmer of violet flashed in the pane as if to whisper a secret reminder. Johan gave a low laugh and felt for the black bone in his belt. Shivering from its electric sensation, he nodded his head toward the pane; of course, there was always her.

❦

Limping past the gaps in the outer row of empty homes, Johan pulled the brim of Dr. Lasser's black hat over his brow, having changed into the young man's set of dining clothes. His cane, hooked inside the waist of an already tight pair of slacks, seemed intent on wracking his knee with each step. Johan straightened out and took a breath, then squeezed his black bone for a little spurt of vigor. As long as he kept his distance and remained unnoticed, he should make it past the station-town without complication.

Emerging from around the last of the porches, he glared at the pale station-town, feeling a nightly wind at his back. Ahead, jutting out like the bow of a sunken ship, lay the outer wall's northeastern corner, alight in torch-fire. Johan clenched his wet palm over the handle of Dr. Lasser's medical bag—inside lay the old tome, his clothes, and a few canned foods. There would be no row of homes to hide behind; he would be out in the open. With a strained gait, he approached, anticipating an alarm or yell. But he went unnoticed. Was no one keeping lookout? Incredulous.

Johan turned at the wall's corner and felt the wind deviate off his back as he looked toward the moonlit hills, their low peaks like an ocean of static waves halted by the air's warm current. His focus returned to the station-town, conscious now of a conversation beyond the wall. He smirked to himself—oh how their eyes would blunder over his figure in the night, faltering and unsure—for only a few meters away, like a sail struggling to unmoor a beached vessel into sea, fluttered the canvas hump of Thomas Dawl's tent. Johan, enthused and tired, hurried into an odd skip, his outstretched hand like an eager spider as it parted the tent's flap.

"Mr. Dawls," he lilted, "Thomas? It's Dr. Mannswell."

The tent appeared unoccupied, the only motion the gentle swaying of a lamp hung from the upper crossbeams.

"Mr. Dawls?" Johan walked to the man's makeshift bar of crates and peeked over. Straw and dirt littered the floor. "I trust you haven't forgotten me, Thomas?"

Empty bottles fell from an alcove in the back.

"Mr. Dawls? Is that you?"

A lanky figure came into view from behind a burlap sack of sprouted potatoes. Thomas stepped forward, slow and unsure, his thin frame much more attenuated and sicklier than before. He looked at Johan, the apple of his neck jerking. Thomas's face had become yellowed and sunken, his eyes large and wet. "Dr. Mannswell?" He gave a hacked cough into his large hand. "A treat to see you again…"

Johan crinkled his nose. "And you, Mr. Dawls. Are you okay?"

Thomas waved the question off and sauntered barefoot to his make-shift bar as he wiped his palm on his dirty slacks. He worked his way to an opened crate and dug his long, emaciated hands into the tufts of packing straw. "More gin for ya, Dr. Mannswell? Haven't had much company past few days…"

Johan took off Dr. Lasser's hat and plopped it on the table, then adjusted his glasses and eyed Thomas with a not altogether magnanimous concern—the man's condition was ghastly. He shook his head and pulled his cane out from the tight leg of Dr. Lasser's dining slacks. Thomas gave a loud snort and came over to the table. He set down a pair of bourbon glasses and filled them to the brim with a healthy pour of Boodles. The men then shared an awkward, dull clink.

Johan took a sip and sighed, the familiar burn of neat gin palliating his nerves. Somewhat comfortable, he pulled his pipe from his vest and began to recharge his bowl.

"You know, day after you arrived," Thomas grumbled, "Mr. Courner's man came to me, asked me about you."

"Oh?" Johan pulled out his book of matches and set them on the table.

"Yeah, wanted to know what kinda man you was. I said, 'very cordial,' I said, 'very polite.' I even told him what you did for them kids. Payin' 'em and all to lug your trunk around. I also let him know that you was lookin' to find your friend…"

Johan nodded absentmindedly and put his pipe in his mouth, igniting a match off the table.

"Kaffer gave me a quid—you believe that?! '*Im*…givin' *me* a tip for helpin' '*im*…my word." Thomas laughed, his face churning into a grotesque mask as he wheezed.

"Mr. Dawls." Johan blew a cloud of smoke into the tent. "That's all very well, but I'm in need of a few provisions at the moment. I was wondering if you could help me."

Thomas blinked as the yellow pallor of his skin sheened with a coat of milky sweat. "Look around ya, Dr. Mannswell. Most my wares is gone."

"Oh, I don't need much, just a pack and a sleeping roll. Perhaps a few canisters of your water." Johan sipped at his gin.

Thomas's eyes drifted over the table. "I'll…see what I's can do, Dr. Mannswell." He rubbed his chin and thought. "You ever find him, by the way? Your friend?"

Johan shook his head, trails of smoke wisping from his nose. "I was led to believe that he'd died. But that was a lie. Although I do know where to find him now. Which is why I need your help. You see, Governor Tuner has it out for me."

"And what for?" Thomas hacked up a glob of phlegm.

Johan closed his eyes in a simper. "Well, as it happens, I've come to realize certain facts that could—oh, how shall I put this—threaten their grip on your township's economy and people...entrepreneurs, such as yourself, Mr. Dawls. Now look, surely you have a few items lying around. Perhaps old field gear bartered off a returning soldier?"

"Dr. Mannswell, I hear ya. I do. But it's trim pickings here these days—"

Johan took his pipe from his mouth and leaned in over the table. "Understand me, Mr. Dawls. I'd like to pay you for what I require. It's a preference I'm offering, not an inquiry of your thoughts on the idea of a transaction. Make no mistake in thinking I've not prepared myself for an alternative route."

Thomas narrowed his eyes and squirmed his lips. He finished the rest of his gin and motioned with a lanky hand for the bottle of Boodles. Johan pushed it forward.

"Oi, Dr. Mannswell...I hear ya. But I'll want all the coin and marks you have..."

Chapter Seven

As dawn approached, a light blue crept along the sky. Somewhere not too far off, a chortle of insects nested in the grasses, and in the air, a hint of damp sage lingered on the breeze. Johan hefted Thomas's Lee-Enfield over his shoulder and scurried down a bushy dip. The long-rifle was heavy, its walnut grip splintered in places.

Before leaving Thomas with enough coin to purchase a storefront in town and the suggestion he procure some rare mutton once the butcher opened, Johan realized the supplies he wanted would be useless unless he found a means of transport to the dig site. Even with his new-found vigor, walking such a distance on foot would be impossible with the amount of water, oil, and food he needed. So a decision had been made. He ate what he could and filled only one canister of lamp oil, whereas the rest would be flasks of water tied to the canvas pack at his back. Stuffed inside were a few canned foods and several tools: a knife, monocle, hip-lantern, matches, compass, rope—everything he would need.

After requesting that Thomas dispose of Dr. Lasser's dinner clothes, Johan had shaken his hand and set off. Lumbering upward, he crested the other side of the slope and caught his breath, staring out over the land. The stars to the west remained white and flickering, unresponsive to the brightening crimson of early morning. He walked over to a lone mokala tree and sat on a large rock. The vantage was good, nestled atop a sloping hill. In the direction of the dig site, Johan caught a streak of purple lightning as it flashed at the murky horizon, indicating the day would bring rain.

He removed his pack and laid the Lee-Enfield against the tree as a light breeze tousled its dry leaves, then took a sip of water and went about preparing a fresh pipe as thoughts of the tome filled his head. The scrap of notepaper bothered him—Karl's rambling of keys, and that word: Ghadra. Johan pulled long at his pipe, rubbing the white stubble at his chin. Arabic, was it? Oh, he supposed such rumination mattered little right now. Soon enough, he would be at the site. Edith would be waiting there for him. To help him. Afterward, there would be plenty of time in which to study Karl's tome. Who knows? Perhaps Karl could divulge the meaning of this whole mess himself?

Thunder rumbled in the distance, cracking through the plain. Johan leered at Thomas's long-rifle set against the tree. Even now, he pictured Hendrik gallivanting around in uniform, stalwart and healthy, the very essence of Germany's rising power in the world. Johan ran his hand through his hair and sighed as he stood up, shouldering his pack. Imagining his son far away in Babylon was a comfort to his heart, and yet a twinge of jealousy floated there too.

Johan shook his head as he grabbed the Lee-Enfield and slung it over his back. He needed to focus. It would still be several hours before he arrived, and if the captain really was in league with Zithembe and the doctor, his approach would have to be one of discretion.

By early afternoon, the sky had festered into a morass of rain clouds and distant thunder. The Karoo was like a shallow marsh; its plains and hills spread in a sheen of rich, coriander brown—dirt turned to clay. Johan wiped his forehead and took a swig of tepid water from the flask at his waist. He lay on his stomach atop a wet hill over-looking the dig site. In the mokala grove below, tapering up through the warped canopy of branches like a pagan steeple, stood the top of Karl's winch. Johan ran his tongue over his teeth and looked through the monocular he had purchased from Thomas. The evidence of a new camp was clear to see; trails of campfire smoke, the milling about of men in khaki uniform, the tail-ends of shouts on the wind.

Johan collapsed the monocular and scuttled back down to his pack. He took another sip of water and stretched his legs out, ignoring the hot mud in his shoes as he dug into his pants for his pocket watch. Waiting until nightfall would be the wisest course of action, but to remain so exposed in the elements any longer might endanger his agenda. Already he was tired and sore, his thoughts too easily lost. With his mind made-up, Johan grabbed the Lee-Enfield and the pack and slowly crept back up the slope toward the top of the hill.

Once more settled on his stomach, Johan gave to scratching his back where the black bone had been held by his belt. Was it really so odd he should have arrived as fast as he did? Oh, it was hard to remember after all that heat and rain, yet had the Karoo not practi-cally folded beneath him as he walked? Propelling him through long distances as if he were possessed of a giant's stride?

A soldier emerged and began to relieve himself on the purple mud. It was strange. From his vantage, Johan could suddenly see the antinatural grove for what it was—a bruise on the skin of an other-wise pristine organism. An ugly blemish in the Karoo. The soldier whistled, sloshing his urine back and forth over the dark earth. Such a vile little insect, spreading its venom without so much as a thought. Johan dragged the Lee-Enfield into his hands and cocked the bolt back. He aimed at the gray sky and fired, the crack loud and booming, rolling outward over the afternoon's quiet pause.

The soldier below jumped and ran into the trees. He was soon replaced by several men scattered at the fringes of the grove. Johan raised his hand and waved as he came down the hill, the long-rifle slung over his shoulder. He motioned again, this time shouting. "Hello! Your captain! I'd request him!"

The soldiers leveled their rifles on him. Johan yelled louder, off the hill now. "Gentlemen!" he said. "Your captain! An audience!" A shot rang out, spilling into the mud at his feet.

"As far as ya go!" One of the soldiers stepped out from between the mokalas, his rifle aimed and steady. "We know who you is! You stay there!"

"Is Captain Rael your commanding officer, here?" Johan asked, the distance between him and the grove no more than thirty meters now. He took another step closer.

"I said that's as far as ya go!" The soldier sidled up, his shoulders stiffening. "You stay there!"

Johan spread his hands in a gesture of compliance and let the Lee-Enfield slink to the ground. "I'm only here to talk."

The soldier remained still, his face and rifle focused. Johan took another two steps forward.

"I said far enough!" The soldier's grip faltered, prompting his sallow fingers to flex and clench about the stock of his rifle. From between the mangled stalks of mokala trees behind him approached Captain Rael, his red coat swaying fast amid powerful strides, a pale hand resting on the butt of his holstered pistol. The captain came up to the soldier and put a hand on the man's shoulder.

"Easy," he said. "You head back in."

The soldier eyed Captain Rael with a look of reverence and relief, maybe even fear. He lowered his rifle, saluted, turned around, and made his way back into the twisted grove. Captain Rael crossed his arms and took several steps toward Johan.

"So," he said, his teeth slightly bared, "never thought Sal would've been so right as to be cautious with you. Where've you been hiding, Doctor?"

Johan held the captain's gaze. "Dr. Lasser's," he said, "and I know why you come to this place as often as you do. I'd like to help."

Captain Rael shifted his lips, fighting off an unwarranted smile.

"I'm supposed to kill you," he said. "I'm supposed to throw you down the pit. Erase you, as it were."

Johan found himself rather amused by the man's innate flourish of command. He gave a nod and listened to the psithurism of the grove. Its mokalas had begun to swell from strong, low-lying wind, making the shade beneath their twisted trunks into a shifting, wine-black floor. Johan returned his gaze to the captain and noted the Englishman's hand still rooted to the butt of his pistol.

"Well." Johan sighed. "If you're to toss me down that hole, I don't believe there's much I could offer in the way of stopping you. However, I'd urge you to consider letting me go of my own accord. I've even brought my own provisions—see?" He gestured with his open palm to the pack and long-rifle at his feet. "We both know it's where I want to be, Captain…"

"Enough." Captain Rael snapped his fingers and juked his head toward Johan. A trio of soldiers advanced, their rifles half-raised. "Take Dr. Mannswell's things to Mr. Rynth's tent and wait for me to inspect their contents. Tell Harris to prepare some food."

Johan eyed the men as they approached, noting the weariness in their features. His Hendrik would never look like that, no matter the severity of the stakes he faced. He would have made a proud soldier. These English were no men, just boys tired of playing camp-out. Johan raised his hands as the soldiers encircled him. One pointed the muzzle of his rifle into Johan's back and nudged him forward. Captain Rael waited with an extended arm until Johan was close enough, and then, like a stern father, he clasped his porcelain fingers around Johan's neck.

"I've no idea how you managed this," he said, "but rest assured I'd very much like to find out. Now, let's get you fed."

As they walked into the ruddy shade of the overhead canopy, Johan was overcome with the subtle motion of the trees, their bent trunks groaning and creaking. Captain Rael removed his hand from Johan's neck as they stepped into the clearing. Karl's winch towered above the excavation like some abandoned monolith created for a long-forgotten purpose.

The captain led Johan toward Karl's old A-frame, joined on

either side by several newer tents. Over by the bench sat a small fire pit, dark. A pair of tired, ill-looking soldiers poked sticks into it, ignoring the tufts of ashen smoke they whipped up in the intermittent breeze crossing the grove.

"How many men are here?" Johan asked.

Captain Rael opened the flaps of Karl's tent and motioned for Johan to enter.

"Don't worry about that," he said. "For now, you're to remain in here."

Johan ducked under the captain's arm and stepped inside. Though not as barren as last time, the tent contained the same cot as before—a cot Karl had slept in. In the back, a desk Karl had written at. Johan noticed Walter's hoof marks imprinted on the tent's molting rug. He turned to the captain, ignoring the sparse containers of munitions and foodstuffs lined along the canvas walls.

"What did you do with Karl's horse? The one I rode here that day?"

"I don't know. Creature probably found a stream up the Karoo." The captain's men met him at the tent and handed over Johan's pack and rifle. Captain Rael entered with Johan's belongings, letting the flap close behind him. "Is there anything dangerous in this pack, Dr. Mannswell? Anything I should be wary of?"

Johan eased his stiff body onto the cot, its wooden frame creaking from a prolonged lack of use. "No." His muscles ached with the dull pang of being pulled and stretched beyond their natural limits. Captain Rael went to Karl's desk and began going through Johan's pack, pulling out each item for a cursory inspection. He upended a few tins of food and stacked them beside a jar of pickled vegetables.

"You'll be sure to put my things back, yes?" Johan filled his pipe and regarded the captain with a wry smile.

Captain Rael's head dropped to his chest, the nape of his white neck coated in sweat and grime beneath the black cut of his hair. He turned around, his blue eyes red at the edges. "Dr. Mannswell, a courier arrived from Adlai earlier this morning. Just before dawn, actually. Not only was the letter signed with Governor Tuner's seal, but its contents held some great bearing on a particular subject." He ran a finger under each of his eyes. "That subject being yourself, along with the express order that I see to your disposal."

"Captain. You may try whatever you like, but I assure you, she won't let anything happen to me."

Captain Rael weighed this comment, his jaw jutting out as if he were counting his teeth with his tongue. He continued rummaging through Johan's pack, pulling out the old tome. "And what's this, eh?"

"A book, Captain. It's quite the relic. I'd be careful."

Captain Rael pursed his lips and laid the tome on the desk, wiping his hands on his coat.

"When's the last time you ate?" he said.

"Not since early this morning."

"And you walked all the way here…in what, a few hours?"

"I…suppose I did. Yes."

The captain rubbed his chin and meandered past Johan, poking his head out of the tent flap. "Corporal Boughs," he called, "have Charles heat up that stew from last night." He looked at Johan on the cot. "And bring a pint from my trunk." Letting the flap fall, he stood over Johan, pale and thin. "I'd have you fed and rested before we talk," he said, stern. "You'd be wise to wait for your food before falling asleep…" He turned to go. "And Dr. Mannswell?"

Johan let a weak sigh leave his mouth. "Ja?"

"There will be two men watching this tent at all times. If you try anything, I assure you, this modicum of respect I've shown will turn into something else entirely. I'll strangle you myself. Do you understand?"

Johan peered up into the captain's tired eyes and held the man's gaze. He said nothing but instead lit his pipe. Captain Rael flared his nostrils and tilted his head almost imperceptibly before stalking out of the tent. Johan blew a cloud of smoke and laid down on the cot. He had to play the next few hours carefully. In the meantime, his leg felt soft and malleable, as though it might pleat itself into something denser. Johan looked at his supplies on the desk, taking a mental stock. As much as he disliked it, Captain Rael was right; he needed to eat before allowing himself any kind of prolonged rest. Johan kicked his muddied shoes off and let them drop to the musty rug. With closed eyes, he rubbed his lower leg.

☙❧

The patter of rainfall had grown heavy when a young soldier entered the tent with a steaming tin bowl. He had short blond hair and bright green eyes, and his over-sized khaki uniform cinched into crinkles at the waist. Johan observed the young man as he moved to the desk, pushed the stacked supplies aside, and placed the bowl of stew down. He produced a glass bottle of beer from his deep pocket and turned to look at Johan. There was an odd intelligence in the soldier's face—a ponderous curl at the sides of his mouth that came across as dangerous. The young man carried a peculiar sense of patience about him. Johan shifted on the cot.

"Dr. Mannswell." The soldier spoke in a curt, light tone, his voice gliding and unfettered. "I'm Sapper Lambert. The captain has left his glassware in town, so, unfortunately, you'll have to make do with the bottle." He popped off the lightning stopper with a decisive push of his thumb.

"Sapper…" Johan nodded to himself. "You're an engineer then. Tell me, Sapper Lambert, what's your Christian name?"

"Charles, sir."

"Well, then. Please give Captain Rael my gratitude."

"Of course, Doctor." Charles remained where he was beside the desk, stoic yet cheery. "If you don't mind my prodding," he whispered, "the captain mentioned you might have an answer to all this. He told us you were Karl Rynth's colleague. Is that true?"

Johan smirked. "It is," he croaked. "Karl and I have known each other for almost fifty years."

The young man let a composed grin spread across his lips, his bright green eyes flashing. "Do you think you could help us, then?"

Johan turned his head slightly. "Will Captain Rael be sore at you for talking with me?"

"Not at all," Charles said, his brow furrowing matter-of-factly.

99

He shoved his hands into his deep pockets. "I might be able to get you a new pair of boots. Maybe a spare uniform and some water to wash yourself down with. I'd really like to hear what you have to say, Doctor. This disease, this sickness…well, we'd like very much to get on with it already."

"Sapper Lambert, I'd say you're trying to strike an admittedly uneven bargain with me." Johan narrowed his eyes. "Not to mention, anything I tell you could be hearsay, a lie. Why the olive branch?"

Charles crossed his arms in the same manner as Captain Rael. The boy was diplomatic; was this the gambit, then? An interrogation by this precocious engineer?

"I weigh there's no reason for you to lie, Doctor."

Johan clucked his tongue. "Oh? And why is that?"

Charles grabbed the steaming bowl of stew and handed it to Johan. The young engineer sat on a crate of ammunition across from the cot, elbows on his knees, fingers interlocked at his chin. "Your actions, for example. Now, I mean no offense in saying this, Doctor, but if you or your government were of a mind to undermine our winnings here, I highly doubt it'd be done through the hands of a geriatric saboteur."

Johan stirred the stew with a wooden spoon. "Sapper," he said, "would you mind trading a question for a question?"

Charles furled his mouth downward, congenial. "Not at all."

"Where did you get the meat for this stew?"

"As far as I know, it came from the town."

Johan pursed his lips, looking back down at the brown-gray liquid in his hands. He was reminded of Dr. Lasser and the sheep —the mutton he had eaten at Governor Tuner's. The sickness. Johan put the stew on the floor. "I take it you understand how it works?"

Charles splayed his hands and stood, revealing his calm face. "I know once exposed, you need consistent exposure thereafter—Mr. Rynth and Dr. Lasser said as much." Charles went over to the bottle of beer and warbled its base on the desk. Johan began to consider this boy as more of a cat, playing with him, a dense aura of pleasured patience, as though a nude secret danced just behind his green eyes.

"So, you knew of the exercises." Johan loaded his pipe. "You were part of them yourself, yes?"

Charles grinned, turning his head to the side. "Exercises?"

"The sheep, Sapper—letting them graze by that hole, then hauling them back to town so they could be served for dinner and such."

Charles rubbed his nose, his soft voice reflecting off the taut canvas of the tent. Rain clattered outside, its sound interrupted by the distant rumble of thunder. "Oh, I see." He laughed. "Doctor, I assure you there is no such meat in your stew."

"Son," Johan croaked, "I don't have time for this." He grunted in pain. "Call on your captain, have him"—another grunt—"ask the questions…" His leg pounded like a drum, pulsing, tightening, beating outward against his slacks—the black bone at his belt grating, heating, burning, *melting*.

"Doctor, I only mean to—"

Johan screamed. The left side of his calf splintered outward, a noise that set Charles wide-eyed. "Good God!" He rushed over. "Let me see." Charles pulled out a knife and slit Johan's pants open from the knee down. The young soldier leaned back, partly from the stench, but also from the white line of Johan's fibula—it had emerged from the parted skin of his leg, like a bloodless, swollen smile.

⬥

"I don't know what to do," Harris said. He was the same squat man who had discovered Johan hiding in Karl's tent. The young man sat crouched with longer than average hair for a soldier and a round face littered with pockmarks. "I'd suggest sending for Dr. Lasser, Captain."

Captain Rael stood by the tent flaps with his arms crossed while Charles sat on a crate in the back. Harris lowered Johan's leg back to the cot, having cleaned it. "I've never seen anything like it."

"Dr. Mannswell." Captain Rael ran a hand through his dark, wet hair. "How long did you say this bone was tied to your leg?"

Johan winced. "Maybe a day, probably less."

Charles shifted on the crate in the back of the tent, the sound of his movement cloaked in the hiss of raindrops thrumming hard against the canvas roof. It had grown dim and hoary inside, the heavy clouds having coalesced, thick and swollen above the site. Johan let a gasp as his fibula pulsed. Harris spit-up in his mouth and began to shake. He stood, and with a look that pleaded for release from the confines of the old tent, he hurried out into the rain as Captain Rael waved a dismissing hand.

"Did you know about it?" Johan grimaced. "The bone that Karl found down below?" He flashed his teeth in a spasm. "You know what it does?"

Captain Rael's eyes shone like dull sparks in the gray shade of the tent. "Karl kept it on his belt, kept it wrapped well so as to never chance it touching his skin. He mentioned something about an aura being enough or other."

"Are there more? Did he find more?"

"I only know of the one."

"Ja? You've been down there then? Any of these men in the camp been down there?" Johan was growing frantic.

"Dr. Mannswell." Captain Rael took a step forward, clasping his hands behind his back. "While I'm still deciding on what to do with you, you might be cautious of your tone——"

"Gottverdammt! Have any of your men been down there?" Johan propped himself up, his face sallow and slick with sweat. "I need to know what to expect!"

"And who says you're going down?" Captain Rael lashed out, jutting his calm, tenable face out over the cot, over Johan. "*I* certainly haven't said so. Sapper Lambert? Have you heard me say anything of the sort?"

Charles looked to the floor and shook his head. "No, sir."

"Captain." Johan gasped. "The bone...I have Karl's bone beneath my back...take it out...use a cloth..."

Captain Rael eyed Charles and gave a nod. The young soldier

dug for a kerchief and reached behind Johan's back, where he retrieved the black bone and hastily put it by Johan, who in the gray gloom, beneath the shrill of falling rain, felt for it. He sighed as warmth swooned inside his fingers, through his raw muscles, crawling around his chest—a percussion at his heart! Licking his lips, Johan sat up and slid the black bone into his leg. Its sharp barbs stuck to his exposed fibula as the skin of his calf muscle shuddered and rippled. A pulse electrified all of his body as a calm, gentle collaboration formed within himself, and a smile beamed across his face. A smell of wet grass wafted inside the tent then, swirling on a remarkably low gust of wind, filling the taut canvas with an inflated sense of space. Johan's eyelids drowsed in tandem, drawing shut to the rumble of thunder.

Edith grinned at him in the white rowboat, her lips drawn back to the lobes of her ears, and the crinkles in her pale skin hooking her face into something of a melted wax doll. Johan was still, his arms and legs drawn together. The sky hovered dark and roiling above them, and off at the shores, the deep pine forests encircled them like the peaks of a distant mountain range; the black tower loomed ahead, obscuring all else. How close they had come—oh, it was monstrous, vast, an almost complete negation of color—a monument of looming onyx. It seemed the hues of his own body would puddle down into the hull of the boat and slosh with the current!

Edith rocked her naked hips, her arms raised like a Hindu Goddess, laughing and chortling in a low voice. Johan leaned his head back and stared up at the tall tower. The boat came to a gentle pause as the point of its bow struck the black stone. Edith wrapped her arms around Johan, embracing him, pulling his mouth and nose to the dip in her collar bones. "We're here," she whispered in the tone of a young woman. "I knew I could trust you to know what to do." Then, as if a gruff man. "Now we climb, old chap!"

Johan trembled against her grip. "Oh, stop it!" she barked. "You've come *way* too far now." As he was pulled upward, a myriad of thin, prickled bones splayed out of her skin, each different in color and engaging with another until her legs and arms doubled in length. He gawked, cradled in the crook of her elbow as she climbed the side of the black tower in a manner not unlike that of a Recluse spider. They soon came to the top, going over a wide gap between a pair of colossal merlons that bordered the tower's parapet. She laid him down, and Johan sat ensconced on the stone, stunned, the surface more expansive than the whole of the station-town. Edith passed over him, the colorful old bones toppling off her body, retreating into her as she shrunk to a petite, blond woman again—his Sylvia.

Johan trembled as his eyes widened to take in the enormity of the tower's dark-stoned merlons that stood no less than twenty meters high. Giant blocks of dissenting light!

"Here!" Edith yelled.

Johan stood, wobbling, and squinted, barely able to make her out in the distance. She was tiny but noticeable, beaming like a miniature lily amid the black world spread at her feet. Edith yelled again, her voice bounding. He walked in her direction, her naked body glowing bright, a tint of green at its edges, and he felt a warm yawn of air ribbon down from above as he tilted his head back and saw a boiling black void, swirling with intricate stars of feathery purples and deep, golden reds—places far away. Eons back.

"Johan, come here." Edith's voice hummed, gentle, entreating, ensnaring. He approached her outstretched hand, felt it clasp onto his forearm. She smiled, letting a small laugh escape her tender throat. "That's it, c'mon." Edith's grin broadened, her violet eyes shining like two neon stones imbued with starlight. Johan whimpered and pushed her away. He grabbed his head with both of his hands and moaned.

"Pathetic." She struck out her arm and snatched him by the wrist, handling him like a rag-doll as she pushed him into an opening in the floor and followed after him.

A lantern had been lit, suffusing the tent's soft pallor in a warm, flickering bronze. Johan took-in a lungful of air, cooled by the recent rain. By the state of daylight playing above him, he guessed it was probably late afternoon. He watched the vague shade of rigid branches wave above the tent, crossing over its worn fabric like finger puppets. He eased his tense body and flexed his leg. The pain was gone. Snorting with disbelief, Johan sat up and pulled his knee to his chest, inspecting his lower leg. It was smooth, utterly devoid of trauma. Where was the black bone? Where was the gaping wound from earlier?

He warbled his glasses onto the hook of his nose, unsure of what he was seeing. His leg was visibly younger, the muscle of his calf strong, thick. He peered over the mattress, giving a cursory glance to the mottled rug on the floor, and swung his feet off the cot. A surge of energy squirmed in his body. He felt bottomless, yet filled to the brim, bending and stretching in ways he had thought were decades behind him. He went to the hanging flaps fluttering like drapes and poked his head out. The click of a rifle being cocked stopped him in his tracks. A soldier stood not three meters away, his aim steady.

"You go on back inside, old man."

Johan raised his hands in submission. "Oh. Yes, of course... could you get Captain Rael for me then? I'd like to speak to him."

The soldier remained still, readjusting the stock of his rifle into the nook of his armpit. Johan sighed. The soldier turned his head, his firearm leveled on Johan. "Captain Rael!" he yelled. "German's up!"

Johan took a moment to glance over the dig site. The ground was muddy, and the hole's diameter looked as though it may have grown; it was becoming unstable. He peered up at the winch, itself at a slope. Johan heard sloshing to his right; Captain Rael approached, his crimson officer's coat missing. "I see you're awake," he said, coming up beside him, "and standing..."

"Can your man lower his rifle?"

Captain Rael waved a hand, and the soldier slung his Lee-Enfield over his back with a salute.

"Danke."

Captain Rael narrowed his eyes in the overcast afternoon, sizing Johan up. Was his face of disgust or unease? His usual, self-regaled demeanor was different now. The man was altered.

"Captain, the winch appears to be unstable."

"Yes…so we've all noticed, Doctor. We had quite the unexpected downpour."

"Then I take it you're still undecided about letting me down there."

"Dr. Mannswell." Captain Rael sighed. "Seeing what you did with that bone of yours…" He nodded his head. "Well, perhaps we could chance to glean from each other just what it is we need to do to…correct this."

Chapter Eight

THE TWO MEN SAT INSIDE KARL'S MUSTY TENT AS THE AFTERNOON'S irrecoverable light dimmed around them. Outside, the camp was alight with a spotted parameter of hanging lanterns and a sizeable cooking fire. Johan ignored the chatter of the idle soldiers beyond the canvas and stared into the soft glow of the oil lamp at Karl's desk. He knew this would be his last night above ground—for he was going down with or without the captain's consent—and he sipped at his warm pint, sanguine.

Captain Rael wiped his forehead, hunched over in Karl's writing chair, his back to the desk. "The day we found this place," he said, "we found more than that hole..."

Johan crossed his legs on the cot, barefoot and relaxed. Limber, like a young man. The captain pulled out a bent cigarette from his shirt pocket and snapped a match-head on fire with his thumbnail. "When I told you it looked like something had dug its way out of the ground, I meant it." He took a long breath of his cigarette. "I've been to war, Doctor. I know what it looks like when a man's hands have clawed at the earth in a desperate bid to escape death. Now, the hole, of course, was much smaller than it is now, but at the time of my and Karl's arrival, it was around four meters in diameter. Still quite large—"

"And your point?"

"My point remains the same. The earth was upturned. As if...a large iron ball had risen from the soil...or that's what you'd think, but for the large, tell-tale fingermarks..."

"Fingermarks?"

"Gouges, Dr. Mannswell, in the dirt."

"Had someone fallen in? Perhaps they climbed out."

Captain Rael snickered, flicking ash off his cigarette. "Bottom of that pit out there is a thimble shy of a hundred and twenty meters...so no...no one *climbed out.*"

Johan's head tingled. His breath grew short. It was deeper than St. Paul's Cathedral stood high!

"The story I told you in Sal's study was true—though, I abridged what really happened, what I saw."

Johan lit his pipe and brushed back his white hair, eyeing the captain in the faint flicker of lamplight. Captain Rael's face sheened with sweat beneath the line of his scalp. His blue eyes widened as he whispered, "He already knew it was there, you know?" The captain lifted his face toward Johan. "The bloody sod already knew it was here, and I accompanied him like an unaware child."

"Why do you say that?"

"He led us right over that ridge! Right to the Grove!" The captain spread his arms apart, flippant. "Kept checking his compass and pulling out his journal as if he were making sure of something." He sniffed and pulled the cigarette out of his mouth, then dropped it to the moldy rug and crushed it under his boot.

Johan leaned forward on the cot. "Captain. What did Karl do when the two of you arrived?"

"He started taking measurements of the hole, touching the dirt around it, jotting notes in his journal..."

"Do you know where that journal is?"

"With him, I'd presume."

"Below, then?"

"Yes, along with five of my best men and several crates of

Lyddite. For whatever reason, your friend was very adamant about those crates...and believe me, they're not the kind of parcels you want transporting by way of a bloody winch. Explosive stuff, Lyddite."

Johan held his breath as the captain's shadow lurched and loomed across the tent, dancing with the flame of the lantern. Johan pulled his crossed legs closer to his chest and clasped his wrists about his ankles. Captain Rael bent down and pulled up two more bottles of beer from the crate he had Charles bring in, then tossed one to Johan.

"Now," Captain Rael said with a sigh, "what I wanted to tell you is that I found what made those gouges in the dirt first—those fingermarks. I found it..." His tone fell to dread. "I noticed a trail, you see. Indications of an object having been dragged across the ground..." The captain retreated into his beer a moment. "Yeah, well, so in the grove...northeastern quadrant, I guess you'd say...in the bush, in the shade...it was a man...or the mummified corpse of a man. All thin and brown and twisted...laid face down...dried up and...glistening. Fellow had long, faded white hair sprawled all around him..."

Johan came to the edge of the cot and placed his bare feet on the floor, waiting as the captain fumbled for another cigarette. The captain chortled. "Christ, I yelled! And to his credit, Karl came running. He did. But what I saw in his face when he realized what I'd found..." Captain Rael puffed intently. "It was like a curtain had been drawn over his features. He was suddenly very cool, very calculating. He told me to head back to the station-town and inform Sal of the hole; we would want to cordon the grove. I told him to hell with the *hole*. What about this old corpse?"

"And what did he say?"

"Bloke had me swear to say nothing of it. Said it was the find of the century. I admit I was dazed...that I really wasn't quite right from seeing this...but..."

"Well, what did you do?"

"I left." Captain Rael wiped his nose and flicked the tip of his cigarette. "Yeah, afterward, later into the day, near evening, I came back with a quarter of my men and set them to securing the grove...and Karl?" The captain held his cigarette in his mouth and splayed his hands about him. "He'd already put his tent up. The man had made camp."

"What about the corpse?"

"Gone. I never saw it again. And when I cornered him about it later on, Karl ignored me, refusing to say any more on the matter. He just looked at me..."

Johan furrowed his brow.

"What's really odd, though," Captain Rael continued, "is the young girl."

"Edith?"

"Yeah...pretty thing. Odd, though. Very quiet."

"What do you know of her?"

"Only that not long after we found the old corpse—after it went missing—she showed up, and readily in Karl's service like she'd been there all along." The captain dropped his voice to a whisper. "She's very strange, you know...almost as if you can't get a good look at her. Something of a haze about her, how she moves, what she says."

Johan cleared his throat. "About the dig itself. What was Karl working on? What's down there?"

Captain Rael tilted his head. A sardonic grin curled the ends of his mouth. "I only know that it's big, Doctor. That the very air within it is enough to make us ill."

"But you worked closely with Karl, did you not?"

"Doctor, the moment I realized what that gaping hole in the ground let out, what it did to my men and me, to the town...I wanted no part in it. You really think Heaven's air was meant for the likes of our lungs? Hell's?"

"How soon until you realized what it did? This illness?"

Captain Rael took a long drag on his cigarette. "That you had to inoculate yourself with it regularly? Not long...we began to keep to the site, with Karl and the strange girl. We hurried what business we had in town each day to make it back by sundown." The captain stared at a point past Johan's shoulder, his gaze empty. "Those first few months were hard. We helped Karl with his work, though. Clearing the hole, widening it."

Johan rubbed his chin, concerned.

"After that," Captain Rael said, "Samith showed up and implemented his plan to use crops and livestock as a way of keeping everyone…happy and fed. Rather genius, really."

"And you didn't find Dr. Lasser's arrival rather convenient?"

"Dr. Mannswell." The captain sat upright, like a statue saturated in shadow, his countenance thin. "What brought *you* here? Really?"

Johan took a moment, readjusted himself on the cot, and swallowed. "My wife passed away," he said, "and when I received Karl's letter, I realized I needed a friend. Someone who knew her as I did. My physician agreed. The warm weather, camaraderie, work—an opportunity for a timely sabbatical. Sure to cure my melancholy."

The captain glowered in the chair, his eyes no more than hints of flickering light as the lantern glowed at his back. "I'm sorry to hear that, Doctor. I am. But Karl's letter…was it typewritten?"

A loud, tinny alarm rattled outside. Captain Rael jumped up, looked at Johan, then rushed out of the tent. Johan hurried behind him. Outside, the ground was like a wet sponge at his bare feet. He saw soldiers in position about the hole's diameter, the fire-pit by the bench alight and blazing, casting the site in a stark yellow flare. Johan came up to Captain Rael, who had already grabbed a soldier by the arm.

"Boughs, what is it?"

"City Guard, sir, comin' our way."

"How far?"

"Some ways—'bout fifty from the hill."

"We've time enough then." Captain Rael turned to Johan. "Alright, looks like you're going down sooner than we'd have liked. Hurry and get your things. You'll need to be gone before they arrive."

"What is this?" Johan cocked his head. "Are you being attacked?"

"Sal's personal security. There's at least as many of them as there are of us."

"I don't understand," Johan said. "I thought the soldiers not with you left for the Cape Colony."

"Not every soldier has a reason to go home after the fighting's done, Dr. Mannswell. And the governor has plenty of pull with his purse to make any on the fence think twice. Now get on with it." The captain waved Johan away, flaring his nostrils. "Grab what you need and meet me at the winch."

Johan retreated to the tent and stuffed his supplies back into his pack, hearing the bark of Captain Rael's orders in the background. Johan wiped his forehead as he crammed the last jar of pickled vegetables into the bag and cinched the straps tight. He went over to the cot and pulled on a pair of fresh socks that he had left furled over the metal footboard, then piled his feet into his clean shoes.

"Dr. Mannswell!" It was Charles, yelling from outside.

Johan finished tying his laces and grabbed the pack from the desk.

"Dr. Mannswell!"

Johan pushed aside the canvas flaps as Charles moved into step with him, the pair of them lining up to Captain Rael beside the hole.

"Captain," Johan said, "you're sure the winch is sound enough?"

Captain Rael crossed his arms. "I'm sending down Second Lieutenant Collins, Sapper Lambert, and Guardsman Harris to help you with your supplies."

Johan gave him a bemused look. "But I've got all I—"

"I'm giving you more," the captain said. "I don't know how long you'll be down there, and depending on what the governor wants with us, there's a chance we might not be able to come back for you…" The captain extended his hand. Johan looked him in the eye and grabbed the man's palm.

"Thank you, Captain."

Captain Rael pulled Johan close to him and whispered. "Listen, Zithembe and Samith were tight-knit with Karl. We all were. And we had a plan to end this, but then Karl went missing, and that damned girl fell in with Sal. She's not right. You cannot trust her. You hear me? Find Karl and collapse the hole, Doctor. We have to cut-off the source. Go on now, my part's all played up. Things are about to get busy up here." He turned to Charles. "We've all made our peace. Every one of us would revel in the realization that we helped bring this nightmare to an end! Wouldn't we, Sapper?"

"That we would, sir."

Captain Rael withdrew his hand from Johan's and craned his neck toward the tents by the fire-pit. "Collins! Harris?"

Johan heard a young voice in the distance. "Harris, lift!"

Two soldiers emerged, lugging a large crate between them. Johan recalled Harris, but the other, Collins—now there was a proper soldier, the type rendered on flyers and posters, a living model of structured bellicose: cropped blond hair, clean-shaven, pressed uniform. The boy might even give Hendrik a run for his money.

Collins and Harris came to the edge of the hole and laid their crate down in the mud.

"Sapper Lambert." Captain Rael put a hand on Charles's shoulder. "Man the lift."

Charles saluted and went to one of the slanted pillars, where he unwound a coil of rope leading to the winch's hanging basket. He began to pull it toward him. Shortly, Collins and Harris helped Charles shimmy the basket onto the wet ground by way of four metal rods attached to its corners. The three men then unhinged the lift's front and eased it down into a ramp of sorts. Collins and Harris carried the crate inside as Charles lifted the ramp back into place and heaved them off with a grunt.

Captain Rael gave a signal to a set of soldiers at the opposite side of the hole, near the winch's articulating lever and pully. They began to wind the metal grip, turning the gears—up, over, down, up, over, down. Johan heard the taut whine of stressed rope and uneasy wood as Collins and Harris began their descent into darkness. One of them lit an oil lantern attached to the basket—a late maneuver in lieu of the circumstances. Johan followed them for as long as possible before they disappeared out of sight, swallowed by the mute blanket of unknown. He turned to Captain Rael. "How long does it take, usually?"

Captain Rael swallowed, sniffing the air. "Not as long as you'd think. But if you're in the basket...I'm sure that sense is much different. I'd average the majority of descents take around twenty minutes. Coming up, though, if filled with more than two men, it can take closer to an hour. But don't worry. I've ordered Collins and Harris to disembark once they reach the bottom. Lift'll come back double-speed with nothing in tow."

Johan nodded, still in awe of the hole's depth—one hundred and twenty meters! To imagine the age of whatever edifice or pile lay down there, buried one hundred and twenty meters! Stratigraphic dating alone would set its age well over several hundred thousand millennia—absolute eons! In the steady tweak of the rickety pully, Johan heard the crackle of the campfire by the tents, the muted clops of horses grazing out of sight in the sickly grove—the nervous coughs of ready soldiers.

"The men you sent down," Johan said, "they've gone before?"

Captain Rael eyed the border of the camp, watching the sway of branches as the hanging lanterns cast a spectral hue into the grove. "They have."

"But you've not." Johan shimmied the straps of his pack some.

"No, Dr. Mannswell. I have not. And I never intend to."

"I see. Captain?"

"What is it?"

"Why did you ask if Karl's letter had been typewritten?"

Captain Rael turned to Johan, his face set like cold marble. "Of all the questions...surely your old colleague would've spared the time to summon you in his own hand, would he not?"

"Captain!" Sergeant Boughs called from the edge of the camp. "City Guard's out beyond! Courier sent ahead's informed us Mr. Courner is accompanying them! He wishes to speak with you! Orders?"

Captain Rael pinched his eyes. "Let him through, Sergeant!"

"What does he want?" Johan asked.

"He wants in...bloke knows you're here. As soon as that lift is back up top, you get on it—hear that, Sapper? As soon as it's back up top, you take the doctor down with you! Understand?"

"Oi!"

Captain Rael put his hand on the butt of his pistol as the sound of sloshing feet came from the grove. Adlai appeared in his mauve duster, flanked by several men in dark cloaks. Zithembe sidled up beside him, tall and stoic, as Governor Tuner came from beyond and parted through the group of men. He whipped aside the red cape at his back and revealed a small package under his arm.

"Dr. Mannswell!" he said. "How very fine to see you here. Just the man we're looking for."

Captain Rael lifted his chin at the package in the governor's hand. "Are you delivering now, Sal?"

Governor Tuner smiled and shook his head. "Otto, always so flippant. This concerns you as well, you know. My patience is at its peak. Tell me, why isn't our German friend in a mound somewhere? I trust you got Adlai's letter." He handed the package to one of the cloaked men beside him. "Take that to the captain, will you?"

Johan watched as the man approached, his steps heavy and precise.

"I'd like you to open it, Dr. Mannswell," Captain Rael said, his voice low, "as I'd prefer a free hand."

The cloaked man came up to them, tall and thick with sunken eyes. Johan stepped forward and put out his hands as the hooded man looked him over, then gave him the wrapped package and retreated.

"Go on," the governor said, "open it!"

Johan tore at the wax paper and lifted the vinyl box's lid. Peeking at the item inside, he dropped the package to the ground and lurched back. "Scheisse!"

"What is it?" Captain Rael asked.

"It's an arm…"

"What is this, Sal?" The captain tightened his grip on the pistol at his waist.

"Why, it's Mr. Dawls, of course. Or at least what we could fit. I had him drawn and quartered for treason."

"Treason in what sense?"

"He aided Dr. Mannswell by giving him supplies, Otto. And as I received no word from you, I thought it fitting I venture out to your little hole and deliver an update myself."

Johan noticed Zithembe stalk quietly into a position behind Adlai, his hands at his sides.

"But here I see you've had our renegade guest all along. You do know Dr. Lasser is dead, yes? That his murderer is at your side?"

A tiny bell rang atop one of the pillars, cutting through the tense camp. Captain Rael looked to his men by the lever and pully. "Bring it up."

Governor Tuner's jowls trembled as the captain's men wound the winch and the steepled pillars began to sway, uneasy in their soil. "I trust you know what this means, Otto." His voice wavered. "We need this place secured. Are you really willing to endanger our survival? Edith is gone! She's rogue, now! Do you understand? It's in league with the German! What do you think's going to happen if—"

With a swift move of his arm, Captain Rael freed his pistol and fired a bullet into the governor's head, dropping him to the moist ground. Several of the cloaked men darted off into the grove as Zithembe wrapped his arm around Adlai's neck and stuck a knife into his side. The captain holstered his Mark II Enfield and strode through the camp toward Governor Tuner's body. "Stop the rest from getting in here! Boughs! Ready the Maxim! They'll likely be coming from all sides!"

Johan, engendered with a sense of surrealism, peered down into the hole's darkness and felt the rising yawn of its strange air, the putrid stench of it. Was that the faint glimmer of orange lamplight rising? Brightening? Charles grabbed him by the arm as the empty basket lifted out of the black.

"Dr. Mannswell," he said. "I'll see you down and try my best to situate you, but my men and I are needed back topside—we've very little time!"

Johan was pulled back as one of the soldiers stepped up to help with the line, tugging the lift toward the hole's side. Once the ramp had been folded down, Johan was driven inside, jostled around as the winch began to lower. Soon there was darkness to register, rising around him, seeping above him, covering him. He tilted his head back, unable to see the stars for the roiling black clouds of night, the dim lamp on the basket's upper supports flittering like a pallid beacon on a doomed ship.

"It gets narrower farther down," Charles said, his words lilting with unease. "Second Lieutenant Collins and Guardsman Harris are setting up your camp at the moment. I'll do my best to orient you once we're below, but I won't have time to repeat myself. So I hope you listen well."

Johan nodded assent, dismissing the pensive, elegiac young man as the basket slid against an angle in the dirt. He looked up again, past the lantern dangling above them. He could see the surface, barely discernible among the varying degrees of darkness. How strange that above there should gape a large circle of flickering night.

"How much farther?" Johan asked. "I feel we should—"

The basket stopped, sending them clambering for a hold. They swayed, bumping against the sides of the chasm as flecks of dirt sifted through the air. A series of muffled yells cascaded downward from the grove.

"Bloody hell. That's not normal," Charles whispered. "We've more to go. Why'd they stop?"

A loud crack reverberated above them. Johan stared, squinting. It was hard to tell in the dark, but it appeared one of the pillars had slid out of its anchor. The basket began to twist and turn in a slow pirouette as the cable started winding in on itself.

"I think the winch is compromised," Johan said. "Can we jump?"

"It's far, Dr. Mannswell. I don't chance it."

The two of them heard faint shouts from the surface then, intertwining with the mewl of the cable that creaked and sighed above their heads.

"The bell line?"

"It's pulled too tight." Charles grunted, reaching toward the lantern. "It's snagged around the main cable—"

The basket lurched again. Above roared a thunder of shouts and ricocheted snaps.

"Gunfire," Charles said. All at once, they were dropped, the wooden basket scraping and bashing along the dirt walls. Johan spread his arms out and gripped either side of the basket. His heart pounding, he leaped, reaching out with his limbs, and felt his shoe sink shin-deep into the soil, grinding his momentum to a slow vertical slide. The basket plummeted below him and crashed into pieces, its lantern clapping as the support beams folded in, breaking and spilling oil and flame over a mangle of wooden boards. Johan hung stuck to the side of the chasm, the soft dirt cold and moist in his hands.

"Sapper!" he yelled. "Are you hurt?" He could see the bottom of the hole now, the light of spreading fire glowing crisp and sharp in the pure black. What was it—three, four meters? Johan pushed off, reeling away from the cold earth. A rush of air flapped at his temples as he landed beside the flaming basket, scattering broken debris.

The outstretched arm of Charles lay bare beneath a plank of wood. Johan grabbed his wrist and felt for a pulse. He shook his head and cleared away the boards, lifting Charles up and out. The boy was still breathing.

"Alright, Sapper." Johan slung the limp soldier's arm around his neck. "Not the softest of landings, but we made it, ja? We're here..."

Charles groaned as Johan maneuvered them off the basket, away from the petering flames. Was that torchlight flickering off the dirt before him? A deep draft at his back? Johan pivoted, turning around to find himself below a large, crudely carved archway—one supported by thick wooden beams that led off into a large, sloping tunnel. Oh, it was grand! Spectacular in its size! The tunnel walls curved on as far as he could see, lit on each side by a row of low, sporadic torches, all easing downward. He stared up in awe. The arched ceiling carved from the dirt was probably twenty meters high itself! No group of men could have done this, not this far down, not this far *straight* down.

Johan shifted Charles's weight as a pattering of feet bounded toward him from somewhere down the tunnel. Soon, the squat shadows of Collins and Harris colored the coruscating walls, as though ghoulish emissaries had been sent on behalf of their bodies. The small lanterns at their waists bobbed and clattered as they jogged into view.

"We heard it!" Harris yelled. "A crash!" The pair came to rest in front of Johan and Charles.

"Is Lambert alright?" Collins asked, catching his breath. "My God, the basket. Harris, take a look!"

Collins moved to take Charles from Johan's shoulder as Harris shuffled to the smoldering ruin of crumpled wood. "I think we'll need to bind his legs," Collins said, "…camp's not very far." He hiked the sapper's arm around his neck. "Just a little over ten meters on through the tunnel…then down we go…"

Johan kept his silence, admittedly surprised. Karl's discovery led farther down? Beyond this colossal shaft?

"Mr. Rynth had a flight of stairs put in. They're quite steep, so we'll have to be careful. Hurry now—we should get going in case that damned cavern caves-in on us."

Johan and Collins walked into the girth of the tunnel, its gradual slope already making itself known.

"What of the guardsman?" Johan asked.

"Harris!" Collins called. "I'm taking Lambert and Dr. Mannswell to the camp. See what you can find out from above. I believe Mr. Rynth had a box put somewhere around here with those Oriental paper lanterns inside. Find them and send one up with an S.O.S., yeah?"

"But—"

"Harris, please! That's an order! Yeah? Good. Now, we'll see you shortly, old chap. Chin up."

Johan and Collins continued on, the groggy sapper shifting uneasily, limp between them. The torches along the dirt walls licked and hissed, creating odd angles of darkness, a shadowed tapestry of uncertainty. They soon came to the end of the tunnel, its grade giving way to a significant gap leading still farther down. Johan peered over the hand-filed edge and saw more flickering down below. A series of narrow wooden walkways had been set in a zigzagged lay with metal cressets ablaze at their railings, each lower than the last. He took a deep breath.

"Alright, Lieutenant."

They began to descend, careful with the grumbling Charles. While moving down the first walkway, Johan noticed the remains of wooden stairs, broken and smashed below; it would seem Karl had trouble implementing a point of entry here. Johan stared in wonder at the magnitude of hollow dirt around him, lost in the sheer marvel of it.

"Almost there," Collins said. "We'll set Lambert by the fire once we arrive."

Johan gazed ahead, realizing they had trespassed over blocks of black stone; enormous blocks, maybe five-by-five meters in size, all nestled together with such precision and artistry. And did his leg not tingle? Did it not shudder as if an excited hum played through his muscles? It was comfortable to be sure, a soothing warmth—levity. Johan gandered above and saw what appeared to be a sheened curve; the light of the torches and fluttering cressets rebounded off a dark surface high atop their heads.

It took several moments for him to realize it was a ceiling. A vaulted dome that may have been larger than the station-town.

"This way," Collins whispered.

The second lieutenant led Johan over the dark blocks of stone. Johan grew dizzy; it was like the tower in his dream, only around him now, instead of sick stars and rising monoliths with enormous merlons, there were curves of deep soil, and wide, sometimes frantic-looking marks clawed into rocky hide high above.

Collins stopped, and Johan brought himself back to attention. In the center of an unusually broad swathe of onyx flooring lay a large opening. A bright glow emanated from within.

"Camp is down there, Dr. Mannswell."

Johan felt like an ant on a sidewalk. He closed his eyes and again recalled the dream with Edith, the black tower they had climbed, her beaming body, her shoving him into the giant black floor. He let his eyelids open slowly, taking in the flitter of torchlight around him.

Down below, a shallow flight of wooden stairs led to a series of spiraling plateaus the size of passenger cars, each diminishing below the other along a descending curve. Johan spotted the campsite the soldiers had set up for him, just at the foot of the wooden stairs.

This is where he was to be left? On the edge of some unfathomable abyss? Atop this immense plateau? An array of oil lamps had been placed in an upside-down 'L,' presumably to help him identify the ledges. A tent and several stacks of various preserves, as well as wood and fuel for burning, were all neatly stationed against the massive black wall. But left *here*? Hovering above a chasm so deep, so vast and dark, so incessantly *large*?

Collins again led the way down as Johan tried to keep pace with Charles's limp body swaying between them. The wooden staircase expanded at the bottom, and as Johan looked down between the boards, he saw long supports that reached all the way below to the black plateau. There, underneath them in all that space, he realized what they passed through was a finely cut layer of black stone; they were descending into a structure.

"Lieutenant," Johan said, "I don't quite understand what I'm seeing..."

"I've no idea, Dr. Mannswell. Only ever been down here once before and never farther than that first step."

Johan looked at the young soldier, careful to keep his footing on the wobbling staircase. "Step?" he said. "Those...plateaus. The ones going down and around this black wall at our left. They're steps..."

"Yes, Doctor." Collins let out a strained breath.

They reached the bottom of the wooden staircase and felt a gust of cold air. Johan and Collins took Charles to a bedroll left out by the small tent. Collins immediately stoked the fire, then pulled out a knife and began to cut the fabric of Charles's pants. Johan sat down with a grunt and surveyed his surroundings.

Above him, in the middle of the prodigious ceiling, stood the unmistakable outline of a large doorway. Was it not so unlike the type of hatch one might find atop a castle tower? Johan shivered, frozen at the thought. His leg hummed with a low vibration and exuded a warmth that crawled and tingled along his spine. With great effort, he went to the ledge of the giant step and peered down between the cressets and lanterns that marked the drop. It was an endless void below, an interminable black nullity all around, save for the dark wall they clung to like birds on a branch.

Johan looked behind and saw thick spikes hammered into the black stone where the step ended. He wondered: could those spikes have been used as anchors? Would there be spikes like that on every mammoth step? Is that how Karl descended? With rope and leverage? Just how much research could he have really accomplished in the months it must have taken to establish such infrastructures?

Johan gazed back out. He knew they were in a tower or belfry of sorts—how the draft rising from below gave him chills. How long would it take one to get down to the bottom? What was this place? Johan put his hands in his pockets and turned around, tempting the emptiness to reach out and pull him into oblivion. He walked over to Charles and the second lieutenant, the soft fire in its metal pit like tiny embers compared to the gorged darkness.

"How is he?" Johan asked, sitting down.

"I'm not really much of a medical man, but"—Collins bit his lip; he leaned back and sighed—"I'd say his legs are both broken...and it looks like his collar bone is busted as well. We'll need to figure out a way to get him out of here..."

Johan dug into his tattered coat, pulling out his pipe and tobacco. "Lieutenant. What are the chances of your men coming down for us? Really?" He loaded his bowl and struck a match on the black stone. Johan furrowed his brow and struck it again. It seemed this stone was—what? Immune to friction? Impossible. Johan sighed and popped the match head with his thumbnail, noticing how Collins seemed to study him.

A creaking of the stairs turned their heads upward. Harris scrambled down the wooden steps, his lamp rattling at his waist.

"Lieutenant!" he yelled. "Collins! Doctor!" Harris made it to the bottom step and nearly collapsed in front of Johan, panting. "I hung around! Signaled up with them paper lamps! City Guard...they—they started tossing our men down! Flung dead to the bottom! Captain Rael's in the shaft!"

Chapter Nine

THE MEN SAT IN SILENCE ON THE COLD BLACK STONE, EACH STARING off into the campfire as the flames in the cresset whipped and hissed at their backs. A deep draft from below infested every inlet of their bodies—a bone-gnawing chill.

"We should try to conserve the oil in these lamps," Collins said. "There's no telling how long we'll be down here."

"But we have to see!" Harris whined.

Collins shushed him. "We need to begin making plans for long-term occupation. Mr. Rynth has a larger encampment down below. I'm sure there's plenty of supplies left, and there should be some spare mountaineering gear. We should think of a way to get down there."

"And how do you propose we do that?" Harris pursed his mouth, his lips pouty and wet.

Johan stood and brushed off his pants. "I'm going to take a look at these metal rivets in the wall. I'd imagine they serve as a means of descent. Tie a rope here, and a man can propel himself down this step to the next—so on and so forth."

"Well, how do you know each step has one?" Again, Harris, with his pouting mouth.

Johan shifted his hands in his pockets and looked at the young man; maybe it was best to ignore the fellow. He turned to Collins. "Lieutenant, there's a phial of morphia in my bag should your sapper need it. I have to get below. If one of you wants to come with me, I'd be grateful for the company. And any supplies we find are, of course, yours to use as you wish."

"Well, bugger on that!" Harris screeched. "I'm staying right here!"

Collins shook his head, then looked at Johan. "I'll go with you, Doctor."

"Are you soft?" Harris's mouth contorted into a knot of disbelief. "You don't know how far it is! How long you'll be gone! What's *down* there!"

"Harris, what choice do we have? The captain is dead at the bottom of the shaft, and the winch is inoperable. Either way, I'm the senior officer here. We go down to get up. It's as simple as that."

The guardsman's eyes sheened in the firelight; the man appeared to shiver. "I don't wanna be alone up here," he whimpered. "I wanna see my mum, my home…ole Blighty…"

"You will, Harris. I promise. The doctor and I are just going to go down and grab some things, that's all. We'll only be gone a day. I can't imagine it taking any longer than that. In the meantime, you'll need to tend to Charles when he stirs. Keep yourself warm and fed, maybe go back to the chasm and see if you can't get a signal up…"

Harris nodded in solemnity and crossed his arms as if he were huddled amid a blizzard.

"Well, then, it's settled—wunderbar." Johan shifted himself beside the fire. "Now, is anyone hungry? Personally, I could use a drink." He walked over to the tent and dug through the crate of supplies, pushing aside canisters of oil, boxes of ammunition, a saber, tins of food. "Ah, here we are."

At the bottom of the crate, wrapped in canvas, sat a bottle of Klein Constantia. Johan also spotted a bottle of bourbon tucked in the corner but thought better of bringing it out—he and the Lieutenant had a precarious day planned, after all. He stood up and walked back to the soldiers, giving the bottle of wine to Harris.

"Open that, won't you? It might be best to keep busy." Johan patted the man on the shoulder and continued to the ledge, overlooking the spiral of plateaus along his left. All that mattered lay below.

Johan listened as the cold air fluttered and curled around him, splaying his white hair about his scalp. Behind him, the sound of Harris rummaging through rations was muted, muddled as if the black stone were strained to echo the man's movements. Was there reason to feel this black stone could portray malice against them? Like the trees had in the grove above? Johan lit a match and cupped the small flame into his bowl. He pulled hard and exhaled into the darkness, the orange glow of the cresset lighting the pall of his breath. Edith would be waiting for him. She would be pleased to see him. After all, had he not done well to get this far?

❧

The cresset burned low, its light grinding back and forth on the canvas of the tent. Johan sat up and creeped out of his sleeping roll, immediately feeling the cold of the black stone at his palms as he emerged into the oppressive dark. Johan blew into his hands and looked up. A few of the torches placed in the dirt cavern above had gone out. Compared to the enormous step he stood upon, the small wooden stairs and slanted ramps leading back up to the tunnel seemed like crude toys. His ears perked up as he realized he could hear the crackling of the torches—and from all the way down here! Their sound was far more vibrant than any of his or Collins or Harris's voices had ever been in conversation.

Johan rubbed his eyes, convinced the black stone possessed an ired sense of judgment—somehow only welcoming of those inanimate dins garnered in the absence of men. Johan stepped about the plateau in socks, his feet like ice, and saw Collins and Harris asleep in their rolls, the pair having curled close to the fire. He checked on Charles, found him breathing and warm, and then went to the rivet jutting out at the wall, where he squeezed himself between two of the lanterns and let his legs dangle over the ledge.

Why had she not come to him last night? How was he to know

what to do? Edith was supposed to inform him. Johan brought his arms together and rubbed them. Despite her absence, he had to admit that since coming into this structure, however vacuous, however cyclopean, there had been a feeling of contentedness. Johan took in a mouthful of the cold air rising from below and allowed the draft to caress his body. The blackness before him, hiding the hollow dimensions of whatever housed him and the soldiers—it too was calming. Johan gave a sigh and released his senses upon the gentle rush of air, where he was drawn into a lull by the sound of deep water, a sloshing that roiled against the stonework. A whisper in the draft, as light as down, crossed his brow.

"*Johan…*"

His eyes popped open. He knew that tone, that voice, that mixture of feminine competence and masculine debauchery. He fought the shiver edging at his spine and pulled his legs to his chest, away from the edge of the giant step, and away from the whispering voice below.

⚜

Collins huffed. "Okay, easy—yeah, that's good!"

Johan stood beside Harris as the squat soldier released slack on the rope wound about his midriff. Collins descended along the drop of the step; the lantern hung from his waist, beaming on the black stone.

"Alright! I'm down. Dr. Mannswell, you ready?!"

Johan turned to Harris and nodded. Harris rolled up the rope as Collins lit a torch below.

"Okay, Dr. Mannswell," Harris said, his breath already strained, "you remember what we said. Hold the rope tight and—"

"Yes, yes, thank you, Guardsman Harris. I believe I have this."

Johan stepped away and pulled at the knot around his waist, making sure the line ran taut over the rivet in the stone. He leaned back and hopped down, his shoes sliding on the smooth surface as he lightly pushed off and found himself beside Collins, shifting his belt with minor annoyance. He unfastened the rope and called up to Harris.

"I'm down! You may toss the ropes when you're ready."

Johan flexed his shoulders as the line was pulled along the face of the giant step. Oh, how he relished this newfound agility of his. Such response!

Collins approached him with a torch in his hand. "Mr. Rynth appears to have staked a cresset by the side here. It's still wet."

"Perfect." Johan patted the wrinkles in his coat.

Collins went to the cresset and drooped his torch into its large saucer. A pale fire bled into life. The lieutenant returned to Johan's side, each of them unsure as the flames struggled to rise. But soon enough, the black stone sheened, and they felt comfortable approaching the broader edge of the step.

"Lieutenant, see here? Rivet. Let's go ahead and get moving."

Collins turned and called up to Harris. "You've the ropes, Harris?"

"Yeah! Here they come!" Harris tossed two coils, the impact of which sounded like the ominous thud of dead bodies.

🐚

Johan and Collins made their way down over the next few hours, lighting the cressets at each step, each doing his best to ignore the heightening cold at his throat. Oddly, Johan's leg had continued to exude a warmth that not only eased the chill but added a focal of calm to his nerves. Whenever they looked up, they were greeted by the ever-lengthening spectacle of a bronze, dotted curve ascending along the giant black wall. The glow of dim fire curled along the massive onyx steps, and at such an angle, it was mesmerizing. The men could only stare for so long before growing dizzy; they continued on, begrudgingly, ever downward.

When next they stopped to rest, their backs to the wall, the weight of what they were doing had finally seemed to settle.

"Would you like anything to eat?" Collins asked.

"No, thank you." Johan sighed. "I'm fine with water." His chest heaved; it was growing difficult to breathe, as though the air itself was too large for his lungs. He lolled his head toward the lieutenant. "How much farther do you think?"

Collins spoke through a wad of biltong. "I've no idea…"

Johan rubbed his chin, fingering the light beard there.

"Lieutenant, I find it hard to believe that Karl would have made this trek each time he came down here."

Collins swallowed. "How do you mean?"

"Well." Johan scratched his leg. "He was able to implement a winch above the hole and stake rivets into each and every step we've come across so far. Those wooden stairs leading down from the cavern, and all these cressets…Karl was the kind to push what could be done, especially if it made his job easier in the end."

The lieutenant turned his gaze downward and put the half-eaten strip of cured meat into his coat pocket, then wrapped the rest in a fold of wax paper. He lit a thin cigarette between shaky fingers. "Doctor…how did you survive that fall? I've wanted to ask you, but—"

"I was lucky." Johan's glasses flashed in the firelight.

"Ah…" Collins grew quiet and smoked his cigarette. At the pop of an ember in the cresset, he resumed speaking, unable, or unwilling, to rest in silence. "So, you think Mr. Rynth is still alive?"

"I have no idea," Johan said, his tone low and withdrawn. "If you're ready, I'd like to get moving again."

"Sure. Spending a night on these steps doesn't seem wise, does it, Doctor?" Grunting as he rose, Collins craned his neck and stretched the cold out of his limbs.

"I'll take point."

The air was oppressive, almost despotic on his frame; every other bone in his body felt bruised and bent, squeezed and contorted— every bone save the black one in his leg. Johan landed on the next step with a wince as Collins busied himself with lighting the cresset. The young man had been anxious ever since their last break. Johan gave a heavy breath into the darkness and wiped his forehead before whipping the rope off the rivet above. He coiled it as he walked up beside the lieutenant, who stared at something below.

"Dr. Mannswell…I see it. There's a floor."

Johan put his hands in his pockets, relieved to see the faint color of their dull fire glinting off a plain of black stonework beneath. He turned around and looked up at the spiral of steps they had descended. A pattern of orange flecks curled all the way up, circling over their heads in the hazy, coppered glow of the cavern. He smiled, elated and proud, and wondered how the guardsman and sapper were doing.

"I think our best bet," Collins said, "is to leave a lantern at the bottom of this next step, stick together, and sidle along the perimeter of the floor. Once we have a dimension, we can start working our way inward."

"Very well." Johan hefted his pack. "Let's start to our right, then, along the base of the stairwell. It's what I'd have done if I were Karl. The steps are a good point of reference."

Collins placed his lantern on the edge of the step and propelled himself down to the floor. Johan followed. They then edged along the slight curve of the stairway, their hands gliding over the cold black stone. Johan flexed his fingers, trying to calm the vibrations in his body. Still, every part of him felt as though it struggled to stay together, as though his bones intended to explode apart.

He clenched his jaw as he led the way. His shin hit something hard, sending off a reverberated scrape that echoed with a chamber-like acoustic.

"I think we've found it," Johan said, aiming his lamp. The muted husks of crates and barrels lined in neat rows came into view some meters away. They seemed to form part of a barrier around an area covered by rugs. This had to be Karl's camp. So, where was he? Johan looked up; they stood directly beneath the fifth step in the stairwell. In the dim bronze cast off his lamp, the form of a wood-fire stove emerged, nudged tight against the black wall, a bundle of logs piled beside it.

"Doctor," Collins hissed, "look there. An opening. See?"

The pair walked ahead some, then turned into the camp between a narrow gap in the crated border. By the flickering light of his lamp, Johan made out two long wooden tables strewn with instruments and microscopes, as well as a large canvas tent like the one in the grove. There were several chairs, more lanterns, note-books, half-melted candles, demijohns, and over past the opposing section of the crated border, the glint of dark machinery.

Johan strode through the camp, ignoring all else as the soft rugs coddled his steps. Out in the pitch-black, perhaps three meters from the camp-proper, laid an industrial dynamo, its cables and wires thicker than his arms. They were strewn along the stone floor, leading off into a cold unknown. Johan held his lantern up, its glow lost and frail amid such utter black. Again, he fought the rising shiver at his back and watched as Collins periodically ignited a cresset here, a lamp there, the torch in his hand more like a floating sylph as it guided the lieutenant along Karl's maze of organized clutter.

"I don't see a body, Doctor! Mr. Rynth isn't here!"

"I'll be right over!" Johan yelled, his words traveling hollow and empty in the dead air. He looked at the dynamo. Karl had attempted to employ electricity down here—a feat for the books indeed. But without a sizable steam engine, turning the turbines would be impossible. Johan adjusted his glasses in the dark. Regard-less, wherever the cables led off to was surely where Karl's interests had lain. Perhaps he was there, too.

Johan shifted the lantern to his other hand, its flame glossing the quiet machine beside him. As he glared into the sable expanse, preening for a clue, the flicker of two violet points caught his eye. He shook his head. There would be time enough to find out where the cables led to—precisely *what* they led to. For now, he needed to rest, and Collins likely required help setting up.

Johan, a little wary, meandered back to the brightening hub of Karl's camp, confident the dynamo's presence proved the existence of another mechanical lift.

The second lieutenant's timepiece, though somewhat slowed through his own admission, read a quarter past five in the afternoon. Johan paired his pocket watch but reeled his hands a half-hour ahead—an old habit. He set the lieutenant's wristwatch at the end of one of the large tables, beside a series of empty ampules and curled papers. It had taken him and Collins roughly an hour to grow accustomed to the enclosure of crates, walking unannounced among the soft layer of rugs, amid such ample light. In the end, each admitted shyly to the other of the comfort felt at the barricade's presence, its vigilant push-back against the ominous pitch that hovered so relentlessly around them.

Collins had located a pack of climbing gear and began taking stock of Karl's supplies. He found enough kerosene in the demijohns to last several weeks. There were plentiful lines of wick and matches, over two dozen barrels of water, a chest of red wine, close to a hundred kilograms of cured meat, seventy bundles of firewood, and, of course, every crate compiled into the camp's border was filled with canned goods. By the lieutenant's estimate, one's possible tenure could last well over three months—maybe seven, with wise rationing. Such supplies had not been seen by the Queen's men even during the war.

After a dinner of bean soup, Collins had slunk off to sleep in a small A-frame he set up in a corner between two large lanterns. The young man was tired; Johan knew that. The boy had done well, and although his presence was missed, there was work to be done. Johan was sure that whatever loneliness came drifting his way would be swept off by the reams of papers and journals stacked within Karl's tent.

He surveyed the radiance of the camp then. Twelve cressets on the outer parameter spaced four meters apart, and ten lamps clustered within. It was more than enough light to beat back that horrid, suffocating darkness. And with the gilded mirrors set behind the pans of burning oil—such proficient use of ancient technique!

Johan put his empty bowl down and wiped at his mouth, wondering what tint the sky was, what degree of warmth carried the soft armada of clouds above. How present the burnt trees and dried grasses were as they sweltered like a dusty sea far over his head. He sighed and packed his pipe, ignoring the chill at his neck. Maybe it was best he wrap himself in a blanket and begin on Karl's notes before he grew too tired. With a mouthful of smoke, Johan rose from the table and made for Karl's tent, its stretch of canvas resting wide and white amid the ranks of auburn rugs. He moved about slow between the long tables at either side of him, eyeing their cluster of tools and instruments.

Once inside, he felt he might as well be back in the grove. Everything was the same, down to the position of the cot and desk. Johan grabbed a cold quilt from the cot and settled into Karl's chair, a little apprehensive at the number of journals and papers piled amid the desktop. He pulled on his pipe and maneuvered a leather notebook from between a stack of yellow parchment, then flipped through the pages, catching dates and doodles—most of which appeared illegible—before swapping the journal for another.

Over the course of an hour, he found that Karl's method of cataloging had grown far removed from the society's. It was at times hyper-precise, with barometer readings, hourly changes in the temperature, and a relatively conservative approach toward his stratigraphic dating. At other times it was sloppy, and the pages of data would flounder, often receding into a frantic script of hurried musings and broken observation. It was late when Johan found a leather-bound volume which contained a legible sheet of the latter:

...bones and castles, my Ghadras. He likes the haunt of his privilege. But I too know, and I'll not abide him now. I have played along for too long. Does he really think I'd forgotten they are one and the same? I've studied him, and I found him, even helped him. But I knew he was like a parasite, having built his many homes on the backs of others, pilfering what he alone knows is below—his precious keys—taking whatever form he feels suggests success throughout the long years. And after I spent my life searching for him! I should have left it alone. I should have left his dried corpse in the grove. But the fault is my own. I can only hope Zithembe and the Sri Lankan keep our bargain, now...

. . .

132

...at off moments, I hear the earth crowd the depths of those dark corridors below, though perhaps because of my size I feel it more than anything else, like an insect fallen to the floor of a house, thrown off the ground at the percussion of a giant's gait. How this thunder booms! Thumping, thumping, thumping...

※

After a few hours of fitful tossing, Johan rose and brewed a pot of stale coffee over the wood-fire stove. He brought a steaming mug to the lieutenant's tent and roused him. Soon, each was holding a lantern and focused on the trail of thick cables that led from Karl's industrial dynamo. Their walk took them over half an hour into an unknown dark.

"I don't understand," Collins said, "the cables...they just..." He froze in place, the lantern in his upraised hand flickering violently as a stiff breeze assailed them. The tangle of electric cables had dropped out of sight, vanished at their feet. Johan came beside the soldier and angled his lantern high, illuminating the massive maw of an archway far above, cut immaculately into the black stonework, perhaps twelve meters tall and maybe five wide.

"Lieutenant," Johan whispered, "do you see that? Down below...the cables..." He lowered his light, and each understood in his own way the finite limits of a man's existence. They were standing before the entrance of a finely chiseled passageway—a passageway that led down.

Chapter Ten

Johan rested at one of the long tables with Karl's papers and journals in front of him. Collins had long ago receded into his A-frame, the young man's knack for conversation depleted. Johan rotated his pipe in his hand, ignoring the smoke lifting from his bowl, how it disappeared into the darkness above him. He checked to see if Harris was keeping the torches lit in the cavern above. So far, the cavern lights remained strong.

As for the steps he and the lieutenant had traversed, it seemed that only those cressets at the staircase's base continued to thrive. He was worried about the soldier; Collins's ascent would be arduous, and if Harris failed to keep the upper torches bright, the boy could get disoriented. Going up would no longer be as easy as a simple read of high and low. The lieutenant would need a consistent marker to help him establish direction.

The various fires of the camp cackled around him. Johan crinkled his nose as the cold draft from the archway billowed once more —and with it, a smell. It reminded him of wet fungus or a low-lying bog. He puffed on his pipe, discarded the crisp, sharp odor, and focused instead on the journals and research he had partially organized. In them, Karl made references to the old tome Johan found in Dr. Lasser's bedroom, stating its contents as the reason he chose to excavate near Thatta all those years ago—why, eventually, he came to dig here.

All of Karl's research gravitated around a single subject: a man named Grey Irion. By tracing mentions of old references to arcane scripture to wholly unknown authors, Karl had stumbled upon an organization. The Alabastros. From what Karl recorded, the Alabastros, or, later, Alabaster Group, was a long-standing entity going as far back as 1211. But it seemed like more of a religious sect —an order of pseudo-science and alchemy, really. Karl, over time, had somehow managed to correlate the Alabastros with events all over Europe—spurts of technological development, questionable principalities, the total erasure of lesser-known kingdoms, all placed around documented regions of blight and desolation.

Johan tapped his pipe out and looked up from the long table. He stared into the dark, his face stern and tired. A faint glow had begun to rise in the distance, shedding an unnatural emerald over the black stonework of the great floor. A small figure emerged at the center of the glow, bright like a star and just as far away. The draft grew stronger, billowing hard at the cressets in the camp.

"Edith." Johan stood up, his heart in his throat. How her luminous body reaped such magnificence! Oh, but why did she stop halfway? Johan strode the length of the table, panting beyond the flailing fire of the torches and cressets, beyond the gilded mirrors and rugs. He then paused, aware of the sheer openness around him, creeping over his frail figure—a moment of uncertainty; should he remain so naked and cold out here? Without even so much as a candle? But she was extending an arm to him, waving him over! She was here to tell him what to do, now that he had arrived. Johan looked back at the camp and considered the sleeping lieutenant. What would become of the young man were he to go with her now?

"*Johan,*" her voice cooed as she swarmed past him, around him, "*come…it's time.*"

His right leg urged him toward the preternatural light.

"*Johan…*" She taunted him with a winnow of her neck, her shoulders poised like a mannequin in a window.

"I...I need a coat," Johan said, unsure of his voice in the hollow darkness.

A sultry titter came to his ears, as if her lips were at his cheek, laughing low. *"So, the old man needs a coat?"* She laughed again, chortling her voice low and guttural, dripping with an echo unusual to the stone. *"Come and go down, old man...you said you would..."*

The light of her body winked out, leaving a stain on his vision. The sound of the crackling cressets returned, their warm oranges and jumps of yellow at the black floor bringing a calm sobriety to his pounding head. Johan crossed his arms and hugged himself as the cold draft from the grand archway billowed once more. He cast a glance to his boots and slid his foot back toward his body. Wary, he hurried back to the safety of the camp and wedged himself between the long tables. Cocooned amid the warmth and firelight, Johan refreshed his pipe and poured a glass of bourbon, ignoring how his hands shook. As he was brought to a calm, he began to sift through Karl's journals once more.

❧

Sometime before midnight, Johan retreated into Karl's tent to avoid the chill emanating from the archway as he settled at the desk. Despite the welling sleep at his eyes, he felt he had finally organized the mound of journals into a semblance of chronology, in so far as the order Karl had utilized them in. Putting aside the initial, already-perused quintet, Johan opened the sixth and turned the knob at the lantern on the desk. A bright swath of light spread over his hands and onto the opened pages of the journal:

...considering the depth of these structures, I can only surmise their age to vastly surpass that of every civilization known thus far. Based on the strata, I can again only guess them to have been constructed well into the earliest centuries of d'Omalius d'Halloy's Cretaceous epoch—earlier, perhaps. The artifacts inside Ghadra Nine are not so dissimilar as what might be found within our own homes. For example, there are the remains of furniture and illustrated artwork,

though the latter is in a constant flux of meticulously shifting paint—if indeed it is paint. There is even evidence of established 'levels' in the form of societal occupation, a sense of classism as suggested by the varying contents of the many rooms here within. As with Ghadra Three—though its architecture had only minor differences, presumably due to the region—every item's size is absolutely astounding. What truly mystifies me, though, is the lack of any physical remains. Where are the bodies of the massive race that created these wondrous fortresses? And where...

A snap outside the tent drew Johan's attention away. He held his breath, unsure if the noise warranted getting up to look. The chatter of flickering fire was like the subtle roar of a beach, that controlled vibrato felt in one's chest as the tide crawls along the shore. Johan inhaled and rubbed the back of his neck. What he heard had most likely been the pop of hot oil or the break in a log of wood.

He pushed his glasses up to the bridge of his nose and returned to the journal:

...by my past experience with Ghadra Three. Ghadra Nine, however, seems more advanced and much larger—insomuch as can be judged in comparison to Ghadra Three's number of rooms and halls and adornments. Last week, almost thirty years after the initial incident with Ghadra Three, and with the help of Mr. Irion, I found the first evidence of Magnorum—what I have come to call the Great Race that built these massive onyx cities so long ago. I will attempt to record this find from the beginning—and without the prejudice of emotion presently pumping through my veins. From the start of my camp, which I have located near the base of the Great Tower, and after many weeks of construction, I was able to finally make my way past the second level of Ghadra Nine in no more than an hour due to the wondrous work of our carpentry team. The uppermost hallway, the only one I have been able to cover these past two months while construction continued on the Great Staircase, is approximately two and a half kilometers in length, fifteen meters high, and thirty meters wide; granted, these two latter measurements vary to some degree throughout. But it was there, on the topmost level of the castle,

that I was able to retrieve from the farthest room—the fifth one—several of the smaller paintings adorned at the walls; a feat surely impossible without the help of the many tribesmen Zithembe allowed me. I am grateful for their assistance and wish them a fast recovery in town. As does Governor Tuner, who was very gracious and appreciative of the painting I imparted to him. Now, as I descended that first time to the second level, I remember vividly the shock that ran through me, though admittedly, I was not surprised by the grandeur and size of the halls. Yet everything was double that of the first level. Were it not for Mr. Irion, I doubt I could have located the Great Lift nearly three kilometers south of the stairwell. For not only was the distance much to handle, but the enlarged stone benches and moving tapestries hung to the walls. While hard to discern even with my magnified lamplight, this gave me—I will admit—sensations of unease. I was overcome with sentimental memories, even longings, and yearnings for the safe comforts I'd forgone. I thought of my son, a man now—an accomplished archaeologist in his own right—and I thought of his mother, the letter she sent me informing me of her illness before I located Irion's tome in that Hungarian library. I thought of my old friend, of my betrayal to him. And through one particular painting, whether from its large, moving swirls of ancient dyes…

Johan's heart sunk. Was it so obvious? Had it been so obvious all along? When did they have the time? Was it a moment of weakness shared before Karl left for his dig in Thatta all those years ago? Or was it a continuous—

"Gottverdammt!"

He rose in a rage, flinging the journal to the taut canvas wall. Had it continued? Had she been making a cuckold of him the whole time? Johan heaved and muttered. Sylvia and Karl?

Seething, holding his hand to his chest, Johan noticed a spread of letters freed from their place in the journal on the floor. He bent down and gathered the array of mail but paused as he saw the writing on the envelopes. While sent to various countries, all had the same return address—a familiar address. His and Sylvia's address.

Johan sagged to his knees and allowed the letters to leave his shaking hands. Hendrik was *his* son. *His* and *Sylvia's*.

Right?

❧

"Did you get enough to eat?"

Collins licked the oatmeal off his spoon, his face pale and solemn, sunken.

"Did you sleep okay?"

"Had odd dreams," Collins mumbled.

Johan thrummed his fingers on the table across from the lieutenant. He was getting anxious. The young man was fed, his supplies were tidied up and ready; the soldier needed to leave.

"I've gone ahead and filled up your flasks with water," Johan said, "and I even found you a short ladder that should come in handy while climbing those steps. I figure you can tie one end of your rope over its top step and keep the other about your waist. That way, it'll follow you up to the next step…"

Collins slid the bulb of his spoon around the inner curve of the bowl. He wore a brooding expression on his face.

"Did you hear me?" Johan stared at him.

"Yeah…"

"Well, you should get going soon. You don't want to sleep on those steps, do you?"

The lieutenant let a long sigh, dug through his uniform, and dumped out several cigarettes onto the table. "If I didn't know any better," he grumbled, "I'd say you were almost excited to see me off —here, I know you're running low on tobacco."

Johan furrowed his brow. "Nonsense."

Collins grabbed his pack off the table and hoisted it over his shoulders. "Well…care to see me off?"

Johan pursed his lips and got up from the table to help the soldier with the rest of his supplies. The two were quiet as they walked the dark floor to the giant steps, each conscious of the dim glow in the cavern above their heads.

"Glad Harris is still at it," Collins said, breaking the silence as they reached the stairs. "If we get out, I'll work out a way to fix that winch for you."

Johan knew by the shaky bravado in the young man's voice that he was thinking of the governor's City Guard. Perhaps he was worried they would be waiting in the grove, rifles at the ready.

"Lieutenant." Johan gave an apathetic smile. "You and Guardsman Harris focus on getting yourselves and the sapper out of here. I'll be fine."

Collins paused at the base of the step and picked up his lantern. "Doctor," he said, breathing heavily as he looked up at the array of floundering cressets high above him, "I'll drop the climbing gear down the hole once we reach the surface. I don't know if such a fall will damage it, but if you can get back up the steps...and...we're unable to fix that winch...well, you should be able to scale the sides at any rate..." The lieutenant fell silent, then hooked his lantern to his belt.

Johan extended an arm. "Good luck, Lieutenant. Be sure to tie your line around that ladder. And don't wait too long before refilling your oil."

Collins took Johan's palm into his own and shook it half-heartedly. "You too, Doctor..." The lieutenant mounted the small ladder and tugged on the rope left dangling from the rivet above. He hoisted himself up, and the short ladder bounded behind him, knocking against the black stone.

⁂

Johan checked his pocket watch and looked up at the grand staircase; it was close to noon, and so far, the highest ignited cresset was barely a third of the way up. The lieutenant was making terrible time. Johan flared his nostrils and entertained the idea of calling to the young man but thought better of it—his voice barely carried within the camp itself. Sighing, he scratched his leg and lit one of the cigarettes Collins had left him.

Still pained and morose from Karl's earlier admission, he had spent the past few hours drunkenly flipping back and forth through the pages, as if this signaled the illusion of time's inherent power to reveal what cannot be forgotten. He pulled hard at the cigarette and squeezed his teeth together—despite the disgust in his chest, he could only move forward by returning to that awful passage. Johan ran his hand over his cold face. He needed to understand this place, if only for Edith's benefit:

...informing me of her illness. I thought of my old friend, of our betrayal to him. And through one particular painting, whether from its large, moving swirls of ancient dyes, somehow still imbued with its manner of science, or the shades and hues of the figure flourishing before me, I felt the already considerable melancholy of my soul balloon into such size as to feel as large as the Magnorum! I became petrified, forlorn as I gazed. Still, again, if not by the soothing memory of Hendrik's mother, I might have stayed there until the oil in my lamp petered out, and I was left alone to wonder in darkness, left alone to ponder my life's deeds and disgraces. However, all I recall of the painting is that of a dark, vast ocean; of a silhouette of a large man in flowing, shadowy lines of clothing, which billowed at his back as he stood regal and smiling atop a silvery, rounded block of stone, his hands clasped behind him, soaring. Mr. Irion cautioned I avert my eyes while he led me farther in—the sounds of a fast thrashing blew past me as if the giant flying figure actually moved on the volitant block! I believe it took Mr. Irion and me more than ten minutes to pass the end of it. And each time I am made to face the trek toward the Great Lift, I have turned my gaze from it...

Johan leaned back in the chair, his breath now visible in the cold chill of the great tower. He rubbed his eyes, his pale hands shaking. Several of the camp's cressets had gone out, and although the remaining light was ample, it flickered with a sense of frailty. Johan rose from the table and stretched; his limbs had grown stiff and wintry. He yawned and looked up toward the dim cavern. Collins, by the number of dotted cressets curled along the stairway, had now ascended halfway through the steps.

Johan went to the metal tubs of kerosene by the stove and pulled out a bundle of soaked wood with a pair of blacksmith's tongs, careful as he carried the wet logs into the camp. He administered the wood into the pans and lit them with a match; the fresh warmth of hot, open flame caused him to smile, relax. How long had he been reading? His eyes were heavy, and his breathing shallow. Johan rocked on his heels; it was almost euphoric, this sensation.

"*I don't believe you wish to find him anymore—do you?*"

Johan turned his head slowly, as if unwilling to respond to the voice at the nape of his neck. "And why should I wish to find that man?" he said, his words hoarse, anchored with dread and vexation. "Because of *him*, the past forty years of my life have been a joke!"

"*Oh, come now…*" Edith's tongue rippled along his earlobe. Johan turned his head. "*I hope you know,*" she whispered, her words a duality of resonance fractured at both of his ears, "*that even with that dirty bone in your leg, you'll never make it back on its merit alone…*"

Johan spun around and faced the faint-green visage of Edith's glare. Edith's hand engulfed his neck, her strong thumb pushing up into his jaw.

"*Johan,*" she whispered, her fingers twitching over his skin like a spider in spasm. "*You can do anything with enough of them,*" she said, her tones innocent, feminine, "*even live forever if you choose…but they do run their course, like all good things…like…well, like the cartridges in your guns. Such energy expelled for a single use!*" She clasped hard at his face with her claw-like hands. "*You're going down, and you'll get what Karl took from me. For us, Johan. For what he ruined.*"

Johan quivered in her grip, struggling to hold his bladder. His lips became pursed from the clamp of her fingers as she moved them, shining and hot, over his mouth and nose, eyeing him curiously.

She looked down and smirked at his shoes. "*Remember,*" she chirped, bright and happy, "*you'll need more than just one to get out—even Karl knew that much. Though, he never let them in. He never let them touch his skin. He wore the bones like a charming little insect.*"

She grinned, fluxing like a star. Johan shook, frigid despite the warm urine trickling down his leg.

"*You don't have long, Johan…the moments are ticking…*"

Dwarfed below the archway, its maw barely touched upon by his torch and lantern, Johan shivered. The openness of it, the kilometers upon kilometers of myriad lower levels, and the air of their hollow halls all rushing upward and blasting along the floor of the great tower, funneling along the spiral of giant steps like smoke in a chimney flue; Johan controlled himself and inhaled a lungful of air.

Clearing his throat as he adjusted the lantern at his belt, he raised the sputtering torch in his hand to the onyx stonework around him. The black steps that led down were shallower than those of the Great Tower, though their size still transcended most carriages. Closing his eyes, Johan put a hand on the sturdy railing of Karl's wooden scaffolding, which descended in tandem with the steps of the corridor and eased his body off the cold stone flooring. A length of rope ran downward, strung through a series of metal clips hammered into the black rock—a guiding grip for the hands. Johan looked at the small, sunken glow of Karl's camp behind him. He swallowed and grabbed the line, feeling its cold fibers tickle his swaying palm.

He stepped down the first ramp and heard the scaffolding creak as he moved to steady himself. Eventually, he began to walk, passing above the tapered ends of the dynamo's cables. As he continued to descend, his torch and lantern filling the arched tunnel with their bronze, yellowed glows, he tried picturing the appearance of the builders, the inhabitants of this place. Had the archway's tunnel been filled with giant children, running up and down its colossal stairs? How large had they been? The very idea of a race of people possessed of such size, inhabiting this structure of theirs...but he was touching it! Watching it move slowly around him as he trod deeper and deeper inside.

The scaffolding came to an end above the corridor's final step. Johan paused, heard the steady hiss of his waist-lamp, and raised his torch. The reach of its light disappeared beyond the high archway into nothingness. Johan lowered his arm and took a seat on the wooden ramp, trying to settle the sudden pulse in his chest.

Johan bit the nail at his thumb. He would need to go *across* this new, massive dark floor and *down* into the next segment of the archway's corridor to find Karl's Great Lift. But the utter blackness around him, insidious of so many open spaces and hidden angles, stretched on either side of him, into…what? A shudder ran through his spine, and he climbed to his feet, stiff and cold.

Wary, hardly conscious of his actions, Johan stepped off to the giant black floor, his shoes arriving at the stone with a subtle clack. His right leg burned, swelling with a heat that radiated upward into his stomach. Sweat broke out over his brow; the dark pushed on him, hinting at the knowledge of long walls far at the other end of the massive hallway. Its confidentiality ate away at his mind, warping his sense of proportion and direction.

Johan retreated back into the archway and clamored up the wooden ramps, panting, staring at the scaffolding around him, the boards and rope and metal rods all shifting in the flicker of his torch and lantern. He bent down and rubbed his palm over the grain, wanting to *feel* the texture of something organic, something familiar. Beyond, just below the crisscross of metal supports, the vast drop of the giant black steps stared up at him. He plucked one of Collins's cigarettes from his coat pocket and put it into his mouth, brought the teetering torch to his face, and inhaled. The hot tobacco filled his lungs—a momentary respite from the gnawing worry in his chest. Just how long could he hide here, really? Cowering like a child at the base of this walkway?

As he brought the cigarette to his lips, an ungodly crack of thunder boomed beneath him and rattled the wooden scaffolding. In reflex, Johan reached for the guide-rope hammered to the wall and dropped his torch to the black step below. His heart throbbed, beating the breath from his lungs and pushing plumed wisps from his nostrils. He turned to face the wide hallway, the darkness thick and slanting at the weak glow of his lantern. Listening, he wiped his mouth and braved for the hallway.

Ignoring the itch in his imagination—ideas of what could possibly lurk so large in the darkness, ready and nearing, patient and poised to reach out from that darkness. After several minutes, the archway appeared above him again, along with the familiar sight of Karl's scaffolding rising out against its curved wall like a tongue.

⚜

Stepping from out of the corridor onto the second sub-level, Johan was overcome by the reversal in pressure. The enclosed vastness stretched and closed like a wet fabric around his body, albeit dark and unseeable. He could smell it on his skin; soft mold, wafting on cold thermals within the dark, coming at him in crude waves, each stronger and more pungent than the last. Outside of the archway, beside the wooden rail of Karl's ramps and stairs, sat a prim, metal cresset. Relieved, he went to the pans, wet the chalked coals with fresh oil from his canister, and struck a match. He stood at the giddying flames, his somber grin a glistening line of enamel.

For over an hour, he sat hunkered against the black stonework of the great archway, his legs curled to his chest as he stared blankly into the fire of the cresset. The flames were weak and unable to give any clues as to what lay in the dark, but Johan sipped at his water flask and forced himself to eat a strip of biltong. Grudgingly, he slid up the wall, breathing shallow breaths, and moved left down the hallway.

Not long into the dark walk, he noticed a softness beneath his shoes, coming and going at odd intervals; the floor's height changed, raising him, lowering him. He shined his lantern at the ground and found strands of colored twine as thick as his arm splayed out like dyed snakes, then released his hand from the wall, again sinking down to his haunches. How had Karl managed it? This trek into such abyss?

Another boom roared through the giant hall then. Johan clapped his hands to his ears as his right leg shot out with an uncontrollable spasm, as though it wished to flee his body or call attention to whatever pounded along the corridors below. Terrified, he reached out and grappled with his convulsing foot, his teeth clenched. The percussive hit cracked again, louder. Was it getting closer? Another lively pulse, followed by a low, drawn-out baying.

Oh, how it resounded through the hallway, vibrating the dimension-less black stone! Trembling, Johan turned down the flame in his lantern and stared at the far-off light of the cresset, now a small splotch of tittering orange in the dark. The earth-clattering thumps grew in frequency. Johan put a hand to his mouth, terrified of letting loose the scream budding in the back of his mouth.

The cresset's light went out, then vanished with a clank of the pans over the stone floor. Johan wet his pants and went limp as a rotted carrion odor came wafting toward him, hovering on the weighted drafts. Had he really seen the vague outline of an enormous man swipe at the fire? No, that was impossible. The wind was merely strong down here; it was powerful and sporadic.

Johan inhaled, controlling himself. He had to move, get out of the open, cross over the dark floor, and reach the hall's opposing wall. But he also needed to see! The notion of becoming disoriented in this massive labyrinth was a genuine danger; if he missed the Great Lift, his chances of finding a way back without such a land-mark would be nil. Swallowing, Johan brightened the flame in his lantern. A small bronze glow spread before him. Carefully, he rose and stepped forward, past the thick strands of loose twine, where he mounted what he could only surmise to be a meter-high rug. He momentarily thought he detected loose designs in its gutted fabric, but the geometry was too large to really get an idea of what may or may not have been represented. A long, seemingly endless walk passed before his lantern caught the faint movement of a dark ocean, far away and high in the blackness. It was a marvelous paint-ing, with waves that crashed and swelled in dull, moonlit crescents. Johan approached it, mouth agape, ignorant of the jangled noise his overburdened pack chimed into the hall's expanse.

He sidled up to the bottom of the frame; it was thick and of a material like gold, yet rusted with flakes that resembled amber. He moved closer, wanting to touch it; the bottom edge of the frame hung four meters above him. He squinted in the constricted glow, thought this had to be the painting Karl had written of, the one he avoided looking at.

Johan crept along the base of the painting's frame, wondering when his view of the dark, roiling ocean would give way to the adventurous countenance of a large man atop his soaring block of silver. The flame in the small lantern at his waist illuminated an almost living resemblance of churning water, wild and deep. Fathomless. His eyes adjusted, becoming fixated, entranced; it was as if he watched a sordid ballet, each signal of action in the waves a dare, tempting him to believe what he saw—had that been it? Had he seen something above in the grim sky? Disturbing the air above the dark sea as it rushed by with the mass of a god?

The sound was so real! He waited, studying the shades of paint though the glare of his lantern only reached a maximum of five meters or so; he could possibly stretch it to seven if he used the funnel magnifier, but that would only narrow the flame's glow to a point. Johan tussled with the idea, as it was far more reassuring to walk in the swath of a glow rather than follow behind one. He would be unprotected in the yawning darkness, lost but for a light he could only aim and not feel. Johan clenched his jaw and continued beneath the golden, tenebrous border of the painting. For now, he would walk amid the comforting light of his lamp.

Johan took his hand from the wall, steadied himself, and adjusted his lantern. Something down the way caught his eye—a momentary twinkle in the darkness not far ahead. By moving his light around, he found that whatever reflected its orange glare was on the floor— a metallic object, nowhere near big enough to hint it belonged here. Johan quickened his gait, keeping his hand on the wall. In fear, he yelped as his palm suddenly pushed against open air. He faltered, catching himself, frightened by the noise uttered from his own throat, then straightened himself, raising his arm to his pounding heart. Hoping to register all he could, he shined his lantern then. The wall at his right had given way to a sizable square recess. He walked into it some, his shoe knocking against a dense item. Johan lowered his lamp; at his feet lay a porch lantern, the kind used for late-night gatherings.

Wincing, he bent down and lifted the lantern with both hands. Its oil reservoir was dry as a bone, and the wick was burned to a nub —charred. Eager to be in a light brighter than his own, Johan poured a healthy amount of kerosene into the oil bulb and set the unruly lantern down. He then replaced the wick with two of his spares, winding them around one another, and struck a match. A soft, electric blue spread like a dull moonrise over the black stone, pushing back at the hall's darkness. Johan smiled to himself. The glass housing had been tinted and stained—a lantern for gatherings indeed!

As the bright blue licked at his surroundings, Johan noticed the square recess's floor was covered in an odd, silvery material, but otherwise there was nothing inside. He nodded to himself; Karl must have left the lantern as a marker. Could this be it then? The Great Lift?

Johan extinguished the small lamp at his waist and stood before the silvery floor of the alcove. He craned his head and squinted his eyes at the walls before him, confused. Had he missed something? There were no means of control or manipulation here, just an empty square of space. What purpose could such a depression in the hallway serve?

Hoping to get a closer look, he stepped inside, immediately aware that his right foot sank into the unusual material. His eyes widened as a light tickle ran up his leg to his chin, tingling his temples. He quivered, overcome with nausea as the unusual sound of large, humming reeds collapsed around him, penetrating his brain. The ground beneath him dipped, and like a falling star, he plummeted downward as the blue lantern shot from its place on the floor and exploded far above on the high ceiling in a shatter of glinted glass and curled fire.

❦

He gasped awake, expelling the hot remains of half-digested biltong and watery bile into the darkness above him. In the back of his mind, he could sense the Great Lift still in motion; struggling,

148

groggy, confused. He tried to move his body—oh, but it was all so black and blaring around him! His guts seemed to have churned upward into the cavity of his chest! His consciousness close to collapsing again, the Great Lift leveled out and eased to a soft stop as the silvery material around his leg receded. For the briefest of moments, his body floated in the air before it came crashing hard to the floor. Dazed, he heard the whispered whir of those massive, piping reeds again, the feel of the odd material swarming at his foot, around his shoe.

"Nein!" Johan flung himself onto his side, scrambled over the cold floor, and yanked his leg out of the rising semifluid that fingered his heel. The damned floor was going back up! Pivoting onto his back, panting and panicked as he glared into the dark, he could only listen as the disturbing, flute-like hum receded and ultimately came to a rest, like the frilled lungs of some primordial bird having just alighted upon a treacherous mountain peak. Johan lay back on the cold floor and spread his arms out as he inhaled the stale air, the faint odor of stagnant water tinging his nostrils. The atmosphere at his skin held a hint of moisture, and was that not the distant sound of dripping liquid?

He gave a cough and sat up as his heart settled some. Groaning, he reached for the small lantern at his belt and waited for the pounding in his head to cease. As the pain turned to a gentle throb, he tried standing, but a bout of nausea washed over him. His head sloshed as if it contained a shallow tide. Balancing himself, he rubbed the nape of his neck and fumbled for a match, searing his eyes the moment its sulfur point ignited. He carefully touched the flaming match to his lantern and exhaled at the familiar glow. Slowly, he started to gain his bearings.

Upon finding a wall, his nerves settled. Easing against its chilled, black stone, Johan rinsed his mouth out with water and tried to rub away the ringing in his ears. Having calmed, he came to realize the air down here was different. It seemed to taper at his clothes in a more composed attitude than that of the castle's upper levels; its odor was almost sweet like dry moss or a curdled flower. Of course, the walls and ceiling were still too large to feel safe, but he could sense the corridor was narrower than the grand hallways above. The area appeared to serve as a passageway rather than a primary route. Johan sniffed and wrinkled his nose; the odor was pungent, thick in his throat.

Venturing along the left wall, Johan kept his eyes trained ahead. Something about this part of the castle created a placidity within him—but why did the Great Lift bring him here? Surely there were other levels it could have taken him to. Johan thought on the ever-constant sensation in his right leg, of the black bone radiating inside his muscle and sinew. Could his possessing it have granted him a sort of access? Johan paused as he came to a widening in the passageway, the black stone slab of the wall angling away from his hand. The floor was slanted, easing downward in a gradual slope. He unhooked the lantern from his belt and aimed it above his head —nothing but darkness in an infinite, blank cold.

Johan kneeled and rummaged through his pack then, finding his lantern's funnel magnifier. He slid the bronze casing over his lamp's glass housing, clasped the latches, and turned a wing screw, slimming the hinged mirrors inside and focusing the flame's light through the monocular. He got up, patted the dust from his pants, and remised the lantern, its sharp yellow beam highlighting a spot of dirty, pooled water down the way.

Chapter Eleven

JOHAN WALKED WITH THE GRADE, THE BLACK STONE OF THE WALL AT his left now replaced by the jagged angles of un-manicured rock. Was he in a cave? He could smell a gross vapor off the stagnant water, its harsh odor practically scratching at his eyes, licking away at the calm in his head, his phlegmatic mood gradually slinking off as he grew nervous, hesitant, yet ever compelled to move forward. Soon the water puddled at his feet. He thrust his lantern about, hoping to find a path of stone or wood, anything rising above the surface. Yet the sick body of water reached farther than he could see, and with the castle's familiar black walls having seemingly disappeared altogether, he was left alone on the murky shore, a lone beacon of life.

The thought of swimming occurred to him, but after a few more steps—the tepid water at his knees—he sighed, relieved that his shoes continued along a shallow bedrock. Johan kept the lantern high and calmed himself, carefully plodding through the dingy, emerald water. Ahead, his light caught the tell-tale onyx of rising stonework, only, unlike the walls in the upper levels that grew out of view, this had a noticeable top to it—a plateau. The black wall was still several meters off, but it gave him hope that his trek through the rancid water had an end.

Johan sloshed on, tired and afraid that his foot might suddenly drop down a deep crevice. When he reached the structure, he leaned against it, resting his head on its cold, immaculate surface. His arm was sore from the constant vigil of keeping his lantern high; he switched hands and shined its light to the left, then the right. Like everything else inside, the high side of stone extended far beyond what his vision allowed, yet for the first time, he knew the limits of its height. Upon bringing the lantern down to the surface of the water, he noticed, for the briefest of moments, the white reflection of a buoyant object bobbing, no doubt stirred by the frail currents of his trespass. Johan wiped his face and continued through the body of water.

As he advanced, he was met with the sight of a pale rowboat rocking gently in the distance, its curved hull seemingly moored between several ivory stalagmites. He stopped in his tracks. A white rowboat—

Charily, he stepped forward, gawking, his heart throbbing as what laid before him came into full view. The rowboat was nestled, not between a pair of stalagmites, like he thought, but gripped in the curled, skeletal fingers of a giant hand contorted in the water. Johan shined his lantern along the enormous bones and traced them up to the black wall's ledge. The sight dried his mouth as his tongue lolled of its own volition from his parted lips. A faltering breath escaped him; he placed his hand on the cold black stone, sidling toward the boat, stunned as the bronze light of his lantern trembled over the massive fingers, each of their segments as thick and tall as his person—God, the petrified sinews connecting them! Practically stone themselves!

He climbed into the boat, rocking it slightly, and sat like he had in his dreams, staring with disbelief at the slanting timber of wrist and arm—the gargantuan mangle of carpus below the ulna, radius bones resembling the deformed remains of some felled, macabre tree. He wiped his nose with the back of his arm, realizing one of Karl's large party lamps sat dark and dusted at the center of the bow. With shaking hands, he wobbled over and refilled the oil.

Fresh light radiated his surroundings, white and pure. Johan spotted a coil of rope at the stern and saw its other end lead off into the water toward the dark shore—an anchor line. Sore, he rose toward the bow and stepped off into the palm of the submerged hand, bracing himself against one of the giant fingers. The bone was hard and warm on his skin, like a grooved bark. He leveraged himself higher onto the wrist—the rounded grouping of the carpus —and squeezed himself through the oblong space between the arm bones. He climbed to the elbow and the flat stone surface it rested on. Awed, he walked for several meters beside the upper portion of the limb. His eyes narrowed as he came to the shoulder, unsure of what he glimpsed just ahead in the mutable dark.

"Oh, gott…"

He fell to his knees, his mind heaving at the cusp of a welling caprice. Was he really bearing witness to this? Was he really staring at the arched ribs of some massive chest? A neck? A head? But was he not filled with amazement as well? Staring at that mountainous skeleton, lying on its back, its bones layered in lines of calcium; were they not unlike the rings of a tree?

Johan stood and made his way to the spine, where he inspected the vertebrae in a state of reverence. His body tingled upon touching the bones—magnificent, dense, and thick. He was standing within the body of a massive man! Woman! Child! Being! Johan snickered, half-mumbling to himself as he made his way down to the slanted feet of the skeleton. His eyes wide and manic, he pointed his lantern along the shaft of bone, highlighting the metallic wraps of a bracelet about the ankle. The accessory was adorned entirely with small black bones, all run through a glinting ring of what could only be the same silvery material as covered the floor of the Great Lift.

There were skulls with teeth as sharp and long as any prehistoric lizard's, but their form and shape were unlike anything he had ever seen. Menacing and suggestive! Every bone possessed that cobalt black so similar to the one in his leg, their veneers dimpled with those awful, tiny barbs. Johan narrowed his eyes at a spot in the anklet and brought his lamp close. It appeared several of the bones had been removed. He stepped back. Karl must have taken these. But why only some? Were there peculiarities associated with specific bones?

Johan walked to the other side of the platform. To his surprise, it dropped off into the water below. He raised his lamp and discovered a second platform about six meters away, the dim outlines of a giant skeleton lying atop it. Incredible. Was each massive body laid to rest on an individual slab? Slabs as big and long as city blocks?

A loud boom resounded through the tomb, echoing from a level somewhere above. Johan cringed, jumping at the clatter as the force of large objects crashed along an upper corridor. He caught his breath as the noise came to a rumbled end and lifted his lantern. To his left, there ran a narrow set of tied planks—a walkway. Johan ran a hand through his hair and shouldered his pack. If Karl had gone farther, he would too. Johan would prove his worth to Sylvia—to Edith.

The planks sat wide enough, but the way they bowed as he stepped across caused his heart to flutter. He dashed off to the next platform and hurried on to inspect its neighbored skeleton. Hours passed as he navigated a crisscrossed network of planks and bridges, each leading to a supine god whose trinkets of small black bones showed signs of being pilfered by an unknown assailant. Tired and hungry, Johan came to sit beside the colossal skull of a nameless giant. Pulling out the flask of bourbon from his pack, he acquiesced and savored the burn in his gut. He leaned his head against the skull and stared at his lantern.

In the darkness, far away, a hollow percussion hit, like a muted tap. Johan swallowed another sip of bourbon and considered the sound. Water drops? The huff and wheeze of labored breathing came floating through the catacombs then. Johan poised himself and scanned the pitch with the beam of his lamp. Silence, black. He waited, squinted, and swore he caught the dull highlights of a small reflective shine beyond. He stood and took a step toward the weak, pendulous dots of light, unsure of its validity as it disappeared.

Were his senses at fault? Had he imagined it? Johan grabbed his lantern and made for the nearest set of planks. Gauging from the phantom reflections' overall direction, wary of the involuted route needed to get there, Johan maneuvered the platforms and wooden walkways in careful haste.

As he reached where he thought the twinkling lights should be, a lingering hint of human musk filled his nostrils. Johan looked around, set his lantern down on the stone floor, removed the funnel magnifier from around its glass housing. Soon he was covered in a warm swath of pale light. He approached the dead giant on the platform, noting that, like the others, its trinkets of small bones had been removed and rousted about. A low mumbling in the dark made him stop. Johan motioned quietly toward its source—the skeleton's head.

As he neared the skull, he saw it was settled to the side, pointed away from him. Its curved backside had been defaced with a morass of dormant lanterns hung from thick rail spikes that had been hammered straight into the bone. Johan covered his nose. The smell of musk was strong. He raised his light to the hanging lamps, sure that this had been what he saw from so far away; their glass housings brought momentarily back to life from the broad reach of his lantern.

A rustle of clothing caught his ear. The murmur of a dry voice. Johan tightened his fingers over the handle of his lamp and rounded the mountainous cranium. More lanterns hung at its dome, along the brow, and in the eye sockets and nose cavity, but at the mouth, between the upper and lower mandibles, a pile of tousled blankets. A clatter of glass and tin resounded from inside as Johan shined his lamp closer. The blankets were gray, covered in a series of dark-brown stains. Holding his breath, Johan stepped over them and into the hollow of the skull.

"No!" a crackled voice wheezed. "Put it out! Put it out!"

Johan sheathed his lantern into the fold of his coat, startled at the sound of the words. As his eyes adjusted to the gloom, the silhouette of a dirty man cowered beneath a horde of clothes came into view. He was shambling toward a bowed corner of the skull.

"Karl?" Johan whispered, "ich ben's, Johan…" He crouched beside a toppled wood crate and dimmed the lamp. "Macht es dir etwas aus?"

"I…haven't spoken Deutsche in years…" Karl wheezed. "Who are you?"

Johan put his lamp on the crate and peered at the man before him. Karl was emaciated, scared, his face obscured by the mat of a white beard and mussed strands of long peppered hair. Around him, the tattered remains of crusty clothes and empty containers lined the bone floor: shirts, cans, and khaki coats.

"It's me. Johan."

Karl's mouth drooped, and a low croak escaped his throat. "You're…trying to trick me…you wouldn't have come down here… how'd you get down here? Your keys…why use them now? What's happened? No, no, no…I had you beat! We had you beat!" He fidgeted for something beneath his mound of coats, shaken and scared.

Johan edged closer, knocking aside bottles and rubbish with his shoes. "You sent for me, remember? I got your letter."

"I didn't write any letter—why would I send for you?"

Johan's face grew hard at this remark. "Because I'm your friend," he said, "and you asked for my help."

"Oh, no, no, no…" Karl gasped and knocked his dirty hands against his face. "Johan?" He looked up, confused, and began to whimper. "Johan, it's really you? How? I—"

"It's alright." Johan smiled. "It's fine. I got your letter, and I came." Inching closer, Johan kneeled beside Karl. "I was told you had died," he said, "but Edith helped me. She told me the truth. I found the bone you left me…"

"Edith?" Karl yelped. "Edith? Edith? He's got her look still?" Karl battered the side of the skull with his fist, sobbing. "Johan… you have to leave! He's involved you now…oh God, and Hendrik? Tell me! Is he safe?"

Johan reached out with his hand to touch his friend, but Karl let a whimpered howl and lashed out; he scurried back against the wall of the skull and pressed himself flat like a roach. "You've been warped! I never wrote you a letter! *He* did! Ah…he, he must have gotten the address from…" Karl's eyes darted about as he swallowed the rest of his thought.

Johan clasped a hand onto Karl's burly shoulder. "I know about you and Sylvia. I know what you two did. I know of Hendrik. I know of your…correspondence throughout the years." His fingers curled into the worn fabric of Karl's grimy coat. "I won't let you keep it. So you need to give it to me. Give me what you took from Edith, and I'll be on my way."

"You're mad…" Karl growled. "You've no idea what you're involved with. Edith isn't a woman! It's Irion! Don't you see?"

Johan grabbed Karl by the cuff of his ratty shirt, conscious of the pungent odor wafting from his friend. "She chose *me*! For once, *I'm* in favor!"

Karl struggled in Johan's grip but gave up and began to sob. "I'm sorry…I'm sorry, Johan…but Sylvia was touched…she suffered in that apartment of yours, dammit! She would plead with me to send for her! But…I couldn't…and…she waited and waited and waited for me."

"Did she tell *you* why she did it? Why she slit her wrists in our tub?" Johan stuck a fist into Karl's face, knocking his soft mouth. "She didn't say a word to me that night! I came home, and she didn't say a word!" Johan loosened his grip on Karl's shirt and sagged away, his ire deflated in the wake of his grief. He wiped tears from his eyes. "She didn't say a word that night, and yet"—he looked up at Karl—"every word struck true…"

Karl shuffled in his mound of clothes, fidgeting for something.

"I found her in the morning," Johan mumbled, "tub all red, her body—Hendrik hasn't forgiven me…"

"Johan." Karl sat up and crawled toward him. "You have to understand what's happening here. Irion requires a key, a rare key—the bones, Johan. It's the bones! They're keys! Totems with which to access the necrotic technology littered around us! We're just too small to see any of it…" Karl held out his hand and presented a small object wrapped in a kerchief, the size of a pen. "But not all the bones are black," he said. "Their colors only signify which Ghadra they belong to, which...hasps of wonder they unlock..." Karl unwound the cloth. "This one..." he whispered, "I located at the base of a toppled corbel outside Ghadra Three...beneath Thatta." Johan's cheeks contracted as he saw a small rose-colored bone glint in the lamplight. The tiny hairs along its surface were so numerous, so delicate and sharp, they gave the illusion of a soft damask moss.

"It's only a shard," Karl whispered, "probably chipped from a larger specimen...but it led me to places far deeper than I ever imagined—far deeper than any other key I've found!" He wrapped the bone back up and returned it to his coat.

"I don't understand." Johan followed the kerchief as it slipped under Karl's clothes. "Captain Rael, Dr. Lasser—they recalled you with a black bone, the very one you left under the floorboards of your home. You had it wrapped in gauze. They said you carried it on you at all times, tucked in your belt like a sword."

"This is exactly why you weren't meant for digging," Karl said. "You're not bright enough, Johan! You were only *ever* a book man." He gnashed his words as a rivulet of spittle dampened his beard. "I never wrote to you, and I certainly never left a bone for you! You idiot...you've been played for a fool...Irion's inundated his entire body with these keys, replaced his whole skeletal system over the course of—look, I collected several bones myself, but I never touched them. My research all but told me so...and when I discovered I needed a black bone to access more of Ghadra Nine's chambers...this immense undercroft..." Karl looked around him, his face a mien of awe and worry. "I, of course, took Irion's help...until I realized—"

"Cartridges," Johan interrupted, "that's what she compared them to. The bones. As if they could only be used once."

Karl leaned back and chewed his lower lip, his eyes lit points of study. "*He*, Johan. *He*. Supposedly once these ancient bones are touched, they...belong to the one who's touched them. That bone in your leg, it's one of Irion's spares...one he hasn't touched directly..."

"You're saying he put this in my leg? Made it belong to me? Why would he do that?"

"He needs a lackey, Johan! Someone expendable to come down here and retrieve a special key for him. Irion believes Ghadra One can only be accessed if a particular set of keys from the other nine Ghadras have been assembled in the proper tandem. His body is riddled with varying bones dredged from the bowels of underground castles like this one—oh, but he won't risk a single one of them being spent! No...he won't do that. It's how he failed last time..." Karl ran his tongue over his teeth. "Do you have any water?"

"Did you find what he wanted?" Johan asked.

Karl kept his silence, folded his arms around his chest as if protecting the area from Johan's gaze.

"Here." Johan tossed a flask of water Karl's way. "You say spent. I have one of your so-called keys in my leg. I believe I used it on the Great Lift. If these keys can be consumed, or...spent...what happens?"

Karl drank deep and long at the flask. "I don't know, could be you're fine for now," he said, "but overuse it..." Karl wiped his wet beard with his arm and stared blankly at Johan. He grinned in the dull lamplight, his teeth dark and ugly.

"Karl," Johan stood and surveyed the hollow of the skull. "Why are you down here? Where are the captain's men that you came with?"

"Goddammit!" Karl threw the flask of water at Johan. "Have you not been listening? I came down here to prevent Irion from getting what he wants! And those soldiers were supposed to detonate the charges at the base of the chasm! Cut-off the sickness from the world and keep Irion out of here! Are you *mad*? What am I *doing* down here? I'm sacrificing myself by hiding what he needs! He'll never come down here, and if he does, he'll never find me! He'll just keep trying to fish for it with little lovesick fools like you! Johan, you don't realize what'll happen if that fiend reaches Ghadra One in the Antarctic—"

"Why did you trick her, Karl? Was stealing my wife's affection not enough for you? You had to corrupt poor Edith too? You used her!"

"Johan…" Karl's mouth drooped as he stared in disbelief. "Don't be so daft…Edith's not real. You don't know what's at stake here! She's a fabrication stolen from an old sketch!"

"No, she's not." Johan stalked over and flung the various coats and blankets off Karl, revealing a cluster of rotting flesh and bones. Johan stepped back as Karl pressed himself into a tight ball. Grabbing his lantern and turning it high, Johan exposed Karl's bed; the bones around him were off-white, barb-less, and slick with grease. Johan shuddered as he realized they were human, that a decomposed head with a patch of dark hair lay clamped between Karl's thighs; another beside his foot; a third in the corner.

"What did you do?" Johan whispered. "Did you…have you been eating them? What…what have you been doing with them? Are those…the men Captain Rael sent down here with you?"

Karl gagged into his arms as the fetal figure of his dirty body shook and tremored. Disgusted, Johan wangled his shoe into Karl's stomach and flipped him over like a beetle. He dug through Karl's ratty coat, then struck him in the face as Karl's hands gave protest.

"Don't take it to him!" Karl screamed. "Don't take it! Please! Please! I'll have done this for nothing! Nothing! Please! Johan! Please!"

Johan came away with the small red bone and peaked at it through the folds of the kerchief before sticking it in his pocket and raising his lantern.

"Johan! Come back! Please! Don't leave me!"

Chapter Twelve

PAUSED BENEATH THE PALE AURA OF A NIGHT SKY SHINING DOWN upon a pile of wooden remains and the slack configuration of Captain Rael's dead soldiers, Johan stood mesmerized. He could see the round of fresh sky above him—so close now! But Johan looked along the floor of the chasm then and sighed as the doubled-over bodies of Collins and Harris, crumpled one atop the other, came into focus. He had been wondering what became of them since finding poor Charles dead on the great staircase. Johan shrugged and stepped around the shattered boards of the basket, avoiding the pile of dead soldiers. He flopped the stiff figure of Collins off Harris and saw the hilt of a knife in the second lieutenant's midriff; Harris's neck appeared to have been crushed, his tongue lolled. Beside them lay the harness and straps of mountaineering gear—it would seem the pair had gotten into a row over who got to use it first.

His hands over his head, Johan had hammered the pair of sharp picks into the dirt for the last time. He grinned as he crawled over

the lip of the hole and rolled over onto his back. Staring up now at
the warm night sky, basked in the flow of a low-lying wind, Johan
reveled in the sound of insects in the grove.

"I see you retrieved it." A girlish voice lilted above the soft
murmur of dried leaves. "That was good of you, Johan. Very
good..."

Johan turned on his side and sat up with a grunt, the blood
draining from his sweaty face. He could make the silhouette of a
tall, dark figure some meters off amid the mokalas. "Edith?"

"The key. Hurry. Give it to me."

Johan dug into his pocket and held out the red bone he had
taken from Karl. In the bright starlight, the dark figure approached
silently and bent down. A long, pale hand plucked the kerchief from
Johan's outstretched palm and retreated into the folds of a formless
cloak. Johan let his arm fall to the dirt as the dark silhouette stepped
over him, toward the hole.

"Edith...where are you going?" Johan said. "Come lay
with me..."

Through blurred eyes, Johan saw the figure was taller than
Edith, unfamiliar in its gait—but it was her voice in his ears!

"Edith...wait!" Johan clamored to his hands and knees and
crawled after her. "Please! I did what you asked!"

The dark figure turned and seemed to regard him for a
moment. A bored, masculine sigh emanated from its throat, and
with a single bound, it disappeared into the hole.

঵৶ঊ

The afternoon was warm, lazing on the trees with a thick brush of
sunlight. Johan pulled his pipe from his mouth, relinquishing the last
of its blue smoke into the air, watching as it roiled upward like a
sallow cloud into the sky. A weak smile spread over his lips as he
tapped the ash from his bowl onto a small rock beside him, imagining for a moment that he was a giant casually decorating a boul-
der. He peered at the hole in the ground, unsure of what to do; he
had been abandoned.

Maybe if he waited long enough, Edith would return. Perhaps she was just preparing for him. Johan laid back on the ground and stared up at the curled canopy of mokalas, letting the grass tickle his neck. The smile at his lips broadened as his eyes grew heavy, and the trees receded from view. Everywhere about him lay the fetid bodies of Governor Tuner's men, the unfortunate Zithembe among them.

Johan sighed. Perhaps he would just lie here until night came, or until he was a sun-bleached memory haunting the grove, a ghost in the grass, an article whose orbit forever clung to the Karoo—at last, a true local amid the dry wind and ravenous springbok. He laughed to himself as the drowsing sensation of being rowed downriver overcame his limbs, sidling his body back and forth against the ground —oh, he could feel it in his bones!

Acknowledgments

To everyone who helped make this story what it is.
Thank you.
And of course, J. Peters

About the Author

Growing up in the deep south, M. T. Roberts developed an affinity for gothic literature and horror. He currently resides in the Puget Northwest with his partner and cat, and gets around on an old Enfield motorcycle.

His works have been featured in Aberrant Tales, Aberrant Literature Vol. 3, and The Anthology of The Weird West. The Ghost in The Grass is his debut novel.

Also from Aberrant Literature

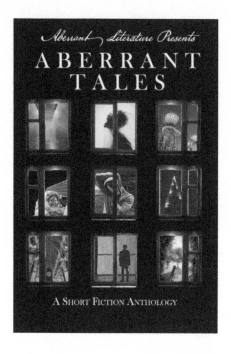

Aberrant Tales is a collection unlike any other. Within this book are a variety of tales bursting at the seams with creativity and wonder. Tales of corporations that allow you to see into your own future. Tales of creatures that dwell within our dreams and nightmares. Tales of gallant knights battling through surreal, gothic landscapes to rescue the ones they love. These are stories that dare to be unique, to have a different point of view. Stories that entertain while conjuring up emotions of fear, excitement, and curiosity.

Aberrant Tales embraces a variety of narratives from the realms of science fiction, fantasy, and horror, and weaves them into one satisfying, eclectic package. Featuring twelve unique tales, *Aberrant Tales* will keep you on your toes as you experience the thrill of careening from one genre to another.

With *Aberrant Tales*, you truly never know what type of story you will encounter next. So prepare to fully immerse yourself in this collection of twelve fascinating tales filled with suspense, intrigue, and imagination. You'll find it to be one hell of a ride.

More from Aberrant Literature

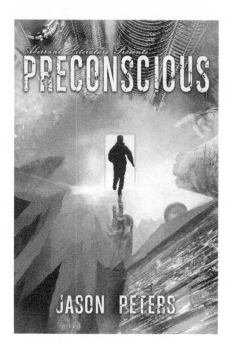

Jim awakens in an unknown room, drenched in sweat and newly amnesiac. As he ventures out to explore the apartment complex, he meets Skeeter, a genial, elderly man who holds the key to unlocking his memory.

Skeeter sends Jim on a metaphysical journey through time and space, with the apartments acting as unique wormholes to fantastic worlds and altered states of being that will ultimately reveal the truth of who he is.

Featuring boundless imagination and colorful, effective prose, Preconscious is a fast-paced, surreal journey that will leave you relentlessly turning the pages until it's mind-bending finale.

More from Aberrant Literature

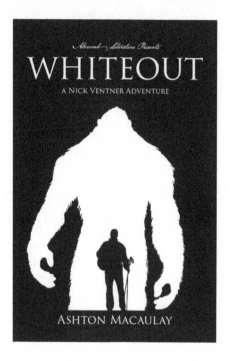

Nick Ventner is a drunk with a blatant disregard for others. He's also damned good at hunting creatures that aren't supposed to exist. From amateur necromancers in the bayou to Sasquatch impersonators in the Pacific Northwest, Nick's seen it all. Even if some of the details might be a little fuzzy.

In *Whiteout*, Nick faces his greatest challenge to date. Accompanied by his trusty mountain guide, Lopsang, and his testy apprentice, James, Nick journeys into the Himalayas to settle a matter of pride and payouts, as he searches for the lost riches of Shangri-La rumored to lie within the mountain's peak.

However, the sudden arrival of Nick's greatest adversary, Manchester, complicates matters, and pits the two in a race towards the top, and both soon find that they have not just one another to contend with, but also a mythical and elusive yeti that has been terrorizing the mountain.

Featuring death-defying obstacles, hair-raising encounters with creatures from beyond, and a heavy dose of sarcasm along the way, Whiteout is sure to satisfy anyone looking for a fast-paced adventure novel brimming with action, suspense, and imagination. Not to mention the occasional whiskey on the rocks.

Made in the USA
Monee, IL
26 January 2021